"Before you leave, hear me out."

Angelo drawled his words softly, playing on Gwenna's hesitation with skill and cool. Blinking, Gwenna focused on him again.

"If sufficient assets are signed over to set against the empty coffers here at Furnridge Leather and you agree to be my mistress, I will withdraw the current charges against your father," Angelo spelled out.

A long shiver ran through her taut, slender body. He wanted a lot—he wanted everything. Mistress? What was that fancy term for? A one-night stand? Was conquest that important to him? Could he really want her that much?

"What does being a mistress encompass?" she pressed without looking at him.

"Pleasing me…" Angelo let the words trail out with exquisite enjoyment.

Dear Reader,

In 2009 Harlequin will celebrate sixty years of providing women with pure reading pleasure.

Since 1973 Harlequin Presents has offered readers a bestselling mix of intense emotion and passionate excitement. Every month you can choose from twelve dramatic and sensual stories in Harlequin Presents and its companion series, Presents Extra, which deliver the ultimate in romantic fantasy and escapism.

Do you like your men ruthless, dark and powerful? Are you passionate behind closed doors? Do you want to travel the world? If so, then Presents and Presents Extra are the series for you!

Happy anniversary,

The Harlequin Presents Editors

Lynne Graham

THE ITALIAN'S INEXPERIENCED MISTRESS

TORONTO • NEW YORK • LONDON
AMSTERDAM • PARIS • SYDNEY • HAMBURG
STOCKHOLM • ATHENS • TOKYO • MILAN • MADRID
PRAGUE • WARSAW • BUDAPEST • AUCKLAND

Copyright © 2009 by Harlequin Books S.A.

ISBN-13: 978-0-373-15094-6

The contents of this book may have been edited from their
original format. The publisher acknowledges the copyright
holders of the individual works as follows:

THE ITALIAN'S INEXPERIENCED MISTRESS
First North American Publication 2007.
Copyright © 2007 by Lynne Graham.

Excerpt from THE BILLIONAIRE'S BRIDE OF VENGEANCE
First North American Publication 2009.
Copyright © 2008 by Miranda Lee.

About the author
Lynne Graham

Born of Irish/Scottish parentage, LYNNE GRAHAM
has lived in Northern Ireland all her life. She and her
brother grew up in a seaside village. She now lives in
a country house surrounded by a woodland garden,
which is wonderfully private.

Lynne first met her husband when she was fourteen.
They married after she completed her degree at
Edinburgh University. Lynne wrote her first book at
fifteen and it was rejected everywhere. She started
writing again when she was at home with her first
child. It took several attempts before she sold her
first book, and she has never forgotten the delight of
seeing that book for sale in the local store.

Lynne, who always wanted a large family, has five
children. Her eldest, and only natural, child is in her
twenties and a university graduate. Her other children,
who are every bit as dear to her heart, are adopted:
two from Sri Lanka and two from Guatemala. In
Lynne's home, this rich and diverse cultural mix adds
a whole extra dimension of interest and discovery to
family life.

The family has two pets: Thomas, a very large and
affectionate black cat, and Daisy, an adorable but not
very bright West Highland white terrier, who loves
being chased by Thomas. At night, dog and cat sleep
together in front of the kitchen stove.

Lynne loves gardening, cooking and collecting
everything from old toys to rock specimens, and she
is crazy about every aspect of Christmas.

CHAPTER ONE

ANGELO RICCARDI climbed out of his limousine, a heavy-duty vehicle armoured with reinforced panels and bulletproof glass, built to withstand a rocket attack. The heat outside was relentless. His sunglasses screening his hard dark gaze from the bright Venezuelan sunlight, he ignored the uneasy chatter of the English intermediary sent to greet him at the airport. While he understood the man's tension he was also irritated by it.

Angelo had not experienced fear since childhood and the shame of it had been beaten out of him. He had known loathing, rage and bitterness, but fear no longer had the power to touch him. His relentless rise to power and influence had featured in hundreds of magazines and newspaper features, but his birth and parentage had always been shrouded in a haze of uncertainty. When he was eighteen he had been told the truth about his ancestry. Any idealistic notions he'd had had died that same day when his chosen career had become a complete impossibility. With every successive year that had passed since then he had grown tougher, colder and more ruthless. He had used his brilliant intellect and razor-sharp instincts to build a huge business empire. That he had not had to break the law to become a billionaire was a harsh source of pride to him.

'There's a colossal security presence here,' his companion, Harding, muttered uneasily.

It was true, Angelo acknowledged. Armed guards were everywhere: on the rooftops of the ranch buildings, in every manicured clump of trees or bushes, their state of alert palpable. 'It should make you feel safe,' Angelo quipped.

'I won't feel safe until I'm back home again,' Harding confided, mopping his round, perspiring face.

Angelo said nothing. He was surprised that such a man had been chosen to act as middleman in a secret meeting. But then, how many outwardly respectable men accepted the kind of undercover favours that forced them into uncomfortable repayments? He strode into the cool air-conditioned interior of the opulent ranch house where a lantern-jawed older man awaited him. Harding was dismissed like a lackey of no consequence, while Angelo was looked over and greeted with a level of respectful curiosity that bordered on awe.

'It is a very great pleasure to meet you, Mr Riccardi,' the older man declared in Italian. 'I'm Salvatore Lenzi. Don Carmelo is eager to see you.'

'How is he?'

The other man grimaced. 'His condition is stable at present but it's unlikely that he has more than a couple of months left.'

Lean, handsome features taut, Angelo nodded. He had thought long and hard before he had agreed to visit and the old man's declining health had provided the spur. The infamous Carmelo Zanetti, head of one of the most notorious crime families in the world, was a stranger to him. Yet Angelo had never been able to forget that the same blood that ran in Carmelo Zanetti's veins ran in his own.

The elderly man lay propped up in a hospital-style bed surrounded by medical equipment. His face was lined with ill health. Breathing stentorously, he feasted his clouded dark gaze on Angelo and sighed. 'I can't tell you that you look like your mother because you don't. Fiorella was tiny…'

Almost imperceptibly the inflexible cast of Angelo's features softened, for his mother had shown him the only tenderness he had ever known. '*Sì…*'

'Your parents were the Romeo and Juliet of their generation,' Don Carmelo recited with caustic humour. 'A Sorello and a Zanetti, not a match made in heaven as far as either family was concerned and the bride and groom were at each other's throats within weeks of the wedding.'

'Is that why my mother ended up scrubbing floors for a living?' Angelo enquired smooth as glass.

The old man was unmoved by the reminder. 'She ended up doing that because she deserted her husband and disowned her family. Who would credit that she was my favourite? It was once my pleasure to spoil her and indulge her every wish.'

'So, my *mamma* was a real Mafia princess?' Angelo sliced in with sardonic bite, unimpressed by the misty fairy-tale aspect of that assurance.

Carmelo Zanetti sent him an impatient look. 'Your *mamma* had the whole world at her feet. And what did she do? She turned her back on all that education and fine breeding and married your father. Compared to us, the Sorellos were *cafoni*…uncouth people. Gino Sorello was a handsome hothead always looking for a fight. She couldn't handle him or his extra-marital activities.'

'How did you deal with the situation?' Angelo was impatient to have the facts that had so far evaded his every attempt to discover them.

'In this family we don't interfere between a man and his wife. When Gino was jailed for the second time, your mother walked out on her marriage. She ran away from her home and her responsibilities as though she was a child.'

'Maybe she felt that she had good cause.'

Dark eyes crackling with grim amusement rested on Angelo. 'And maybe you're in for a surprise or two, because I think you put your precious *mamma* on a pedestal when she died.'

Anger at that insinuation made Angelo turn pale below his bronzed complexion. Only the awareness that Carmelo would revel in getting under his skin kept him silent.

The older man slumped heavily back against the pillows. 'Fiorella was my daughter and dear to my heart, but she shamed and disappointed me when she walked out on her husband.'

'She was twenty-two years old and Sorello was serving a life sentence. Why shouldn't she have sought a fresh start for herself and her child?'

'Loyalty is not negotiable in my world. When Fiorella vanished, people got nervous about how much she might know about certain activities. Her treachery was a stain on Gino's honour as well and it made her many enemies.' Carmelo Zanetti shook his head wearily. 'But she was destroyed by her own ignorance and folly.'

Angelo's attention was keenly focused on the older man. 'Obviously you didn't lose track of my mother and you know what happened to her after she arrived in England.'

'You won't like what I have to tell you.'

'I'll cope,' Angelo said drily.

Carmelo pressed the bell by the bed. 'You'll take a seat and have a glass of wine while we talk. This one time you will behave like my grandson.'

Angelo wanted to deny the relationship but he knew he could not. A certain amount of civility was the price he had to pay for the information he had long sought to make sense of his background. Squaring his broad shoulders, he sat down in a lithe, controlled movement. A manservant brought in a silver tray bearing a single glass filled with ruby liquid and a plate of tiny almond pastries. With a glint of something hidden in his sharp old eyes, Carmelo Zanetti watched the younger man lift the glass and slowly sip.

'How does it feel to have rejected your every living relative?'

A sardonic smile of acknowledgement curved Angelo's handsome sculpted mouth. 'It kept me out of prison…it may even have kept me alive. The family tree is distressingly full of early deaths and unlikely accidents.'

After having taken a moment to absorb that acid response, Don Carmelo succumbed to a choking bout of appreciative laughter. Alarmed by the aftermath in which the old man struggled for breath, Angelo got up to summon assistance only to be irritably waved back to his seat.

'Please tell me about my mother,' Angelo urged.

His companion gave him a mocking look. 'I want you to know that when she left Sardinia, she had money. My late wife had left her amply provided for. Your mother's misfortune was that she had very poor taste in men.'

Angelo tensed.

Carmelo Zanetti gave him a cynical glance. 'I warned you that you wouldn't like it. Of course there was a man involved. An Englishman she met soon after your father went to prison. Why do you think she headed to London when she spoke not a word of English? Her boyfriend promised to marry her when she was free. She changed her name as soon as she arrived and began to plan her divorce.'

'How do you know all this?'

'I have a couple of letters that the boyfriend wrote her. He had no idea who her connections were. Once she was settled he offered to take care of her money, but he took care of it so well that she never saw it again. He bled her dry and I understand he lost it all on the stock market.'

Angelo was very still but his brilliant gaze glittered like black diamonds on ice. 'Is there more?'

'He abandoned her when she was pregnant by him and that was when she discovered that he was already married.'

In shock at that further revelation, Angelo gritted his teeth and was betrayed into comment. 'I had no idea.'

'She lost the baby and never recovered her health.'

'You knew all this…yet you chose not to help her?' Angelo recognised the cold, critical detachment that had ultimately decided his frail mother's fate.

'She could have asked for assistance at any time but she didn't. I will be frank. She had become an embarrassment to us and there were complications. Gino got out of prison on appeal. He wanted you, his son, back and he wanted revenge on his unfaithful wife. Your mother's whereabouts had to remain a secret if you were not to end up in the hands of a violent drunk. Silence kept both of you safe.'

'It didn't stop us going hungry though,' Angelo replied without any inflection.

'You survived—'

'But she didn't,' Angelo incised.

Don Carmelo revealed no regret. 'I'm not a forgiving man. She let the family down and the final insult was her belief that she had to keep her son away from my influence. She got religion before she died and turned against us even more.'

'If you never saw her again, how do you know that?'

The old man grimaced. 'She phoned me when her health

was failing. She was worried about what would happen to you. But she still begged me to respect her wishes and not to claim you when she was gone.'

Angelo could see that exhaustion was steadily claiming the older man and pushing their meeting to a close. 'I appreciate your candour. I would like the name of the man who stole my mother's money.'

'His name was Donald Hamilton.' Don Carmelo lifted a large envelope and extended it. 'The letters. Take them.'

'What happened to him?'

'Nothing.'

'Nothing?' Angelo queried. 'My mother died when I was seven years old.'

'And now here you are, proud not to be a Zanetti or a Sorello. If you are so unlike the stock from which you were bred, why do you want Hamilton's name?' the old man riposted. 'What could you intend to do with it?'

Angelo surveyed him with dark expressionless eyes and shifted a shoulder in an almost infinitesimal shrug.

'Don't do anything foolish, Angelo.'

Angelo laughed out loud. 'I can't believe you're saying that to me.'

'Who better? I've spent the last decade in exile. I've been hunted across this planet by the forces of law and order and by my enemies. But my time is almost up,' Carmelo Zanetti mused. 'You are the closest relative I have left and I have watched over you all your life.'

'Only not so that I noticed,' Angelo countered, unimpressed by the claim.

'Perhaps we are cleverer than you think. You may also find out that, under the skin, you have more in common with us than you want to admit.'

Angelo lifted his arrogant dark head high, strong denial of that suggestion in every inch of his proud bearing. 'No. I really don't think so.'

A basket of flowers on her arm, Gwenna hurried down the muddy lane in pursuit of the two little boys. Thrilled by the growling noises she was making in her role as a pursuing bear, Freddy and Jake were in fits of giggles. With her dog, Piglet, a tiny barrel-shaped mongrel, hard on their heels and barking like mad, they made a noisy trio. The insistent ring of a mobile phone sliced through the laughter. Gwenna fell still and with a guilty air of reluctance dug the item out of her pocket.

'Is that children I hear?' Eva Hamilton demanded sharply. 'Have you let Joyce Miller lumber you with those horrid brats again?'

Giving the twins a pleading glance, Gwenna put a finger to her lips in the universal signal for silence and sidestepped the question. 'I'll be with you in less than an hour—'

'Have you any idea how much still has to be done here?'

'I thought the caterers—'

'I'm talking about the cleaning,' her stepmother cut in acidly.

Gwenna almost flinched for it seemed to her that the past week had passed by in a relentless blur of labour. Even her back, well toned from regular physical activity at the plant nursery where she worked, had developed an ache. 'Did I miss something out?'

'The furniture is getting dusty again and the flowers in the drawing room are drooping,' Eva Hamilton snapped out accusingly. 'I want everything to be perfect tomorrow for your father, so you'll have to see to it all this evening.'

'Yes, of course.' Gwenna reminded herself that the

endless preparation required to stage Eva's buffet lunch for a handful of select guests was in aid of a very good cause. First and foremost, tomorrow was her father's big day. Donald Hamilton had worked tirelessly to raise the funds necessary to begin the restoration of the overgrown gardens of Massey Manor. Although the manor house was virtually derelict, the gardens had been designed by a leading nineteenth-century garden luminary and the village was badly in need of a tourist attraction to stimulate the local economy. A host of local VIPs and the press would be present to record the moment when Donald Hamilton symbolically opened the long padlocked gates of the old estate so that the first phase of the work on the grounds could begin.

'The Evil Witch always steals your smile,' Freddy lamented.

'I'm a bear and bears don't smile,' Gwenna informed him with determined cheer, snapping back into play mode for the boys' benefit. But the children had barely got to loose a delighted giggle at the fearful face she assumed when an outburst of frantic barking gave Gwenna something more pressing to think about.

'Oh no!' she groaned, racing for the village green where Piglet had clearly found a victim. She was furious with herself for letting her pet off the lead. Although the little animal was very loving and terrific with children he had one troublesome quirk. Having been dumped by the roadside by his first owners and injured as a result, Piglet had developed a pronounced antipathy towards cars and was prone to taking an aggressive stance with their male occupants. Fortunately for him, he was so tiny that his belligerence usually struck people as a joke rather than a source of complaint.

'Piglet…no!' Gwenna launched the instant she saw her pet dancing furiously round the very tall dark male standing by the church lychgate.

In spite of the sunshine and his undeniably picturesque and bucolic surroundings, Angelo was not in a good mood. The state-of-the-art satellite-navigation system in the limo, developed by one of his own companies, had proved to be as accurate as a tenth-century map when challenged to deliver the goods in this rural location. His chauffeur had tried to drive down a lane barely wide enough to take a bike and had scratched the limo's paintwork before finally being forced to admit that he was hopelessly lost. While Angelo had climbed out to stretch his legs, his security team were endeavouring to locate another living being in a village so deserted that he would not have been surprised to find out that he had strayed onto the set of a disaster movie. An attempted assault by a freaky mini-dog with enormous rabbit ears and incongruous short legs was no more welcome. As the careless pet owner approached him at a run Angelo had an icy cutting reproof on his lips.

'Piglet…stop that right now!' Gwenna was aghast to see that Piglet had targeted a male dressed in an immaculate business suit, for in her experience such men were less tolerant of annoyances. There were two houses for sale on the other side of the green and she wondered if he was a city estate agent.

Angelo looked down into clear eyes the startling blue of Dutch Delft, set in a heart-shaped face of such rare beauty that for the first time in his life he forgot what he had intended to say. In a millisecond the opportunity to stare was lost. Fair head bowing, she bent down in an effort to catch the offending dog.

'I'm so sorry…please don't move in case you stand on him,' Gwenna begged, frantically chasing her defiant pet round masculine feet shod in the very finest leather. By the time she got a firm hand curved round Piglet's wriggly little body she felt hot and exceedingly foolish.

Out of the corner of his eye Angelo saw one of his security team hurrying towards him to provide the usual if belated barrier between his employer and the rest of the human race. Angelo shifted a staying hand to keep the man at a distance. The rays of the sun were picking out streaks of pure gold in her hair. Even though that blonde waving mass was confined in a band at the nape of her neck, it was still long enough to trail down her narrow spine. In his mind's eye he was still picturing her face and already questioning why she had had such an impact on him. He was fiercely impatient for her to look up again.

'Piglet, you little rascal…I'm so, *so* sorry,' Gwenna declared feverishly, clipping Piglet's lead to his collar and rising. 'He didn't nip you, did he?'

Even while Angelo marvelled at the impact of her beautiful eyes, wide cheekbones and generous mouth, he was also registering that the world of fashion and style was foreign territory to her. Her faded blue summer dress hinted at the lush curve of her breasts before billowing out in shapeless folds that revealed only her slender ankles. 'Nip?' he queried, his lean, powerful frame poised with natural elegance while he waited for her to respond to him as women always responded, with widened eyes and smiles and a host of flirtatious signals.

'Bite? He didn't, did he? He has teeth like needles.' Intimidated by his sheer size, for he was well over six feet in height, Gwenna kept her distance. It was impossible though to avoid noticing how extremely handsome he was. That awareness, not to mention the weird compulsion she had to stare at him, was sufficiently unlike her to make her feel distinctly unsettled in his presence.

'He didn't bite…' Angelo watched and waited in vain for the female sexual response that was so predictable, he expected it and took it for granted. Instead her long silky brown lashes screened her expressive gaze and she evaded his scrutiny. It annoyed him even while he was absorbing the fact that, in spite of the unforgiving brightness of the light, her skin retained the luminescent sheen of a pearl. He wondered if she was that same pale-as-milk shade all over and almost smiled.

'Thank goodness…Jake…Freddy!' Gwenna was anxiously looking back to see where the boys had got to and eager to focus her attention elsewhere.

Two ginger heads popped out from behind the hedge that bounded the grounds of the church.

Angelo froze. She had kids? He scanned her hand. Her wedding finger was bare.

'Chase us, Gwenna!' Freddy begged.

'Are you their nanny?' Angelo enquired.

Gwenna blinked in surprise at that unexpected question. 'No, I'm not…I'm just looking after them for an hour. Excuse me,' she added, glancing up without meaning to and discovering that his dark golden eyes held a light that made her tummy clench and her throat tighten. Hurriedly she screened him out again and grabbed up the basket of flowers that she had set down.

'Perhaps you could tell me how far Peveril House is from here.'

Gwenna came to a halt again, for any appeal for assistance was a sure path to her full attention. She glanced across the green but there was no sign of the car he must have arrived in. 'It's a good five miles. If you go down the fork behind the church, you'll see a sign for the hotel,' she told him. 'People don't often come this way.'

'I wonder why not,' Angelo drawled softly. 'The scenery is quite exquisite. Will you dine with me tonight?'

Taken aback by that smooth invitation, Gwenna flashed him a surprised glance and soft pink warmed her cheeks. 'But I don't know you…'

'Seize the opportunity,' Angelo advised silkily.

'No…thank you, but I can't.'

'Why not?'

Other men invariably retreated at the first hint of refusal. That bold demand for an explanation startled her. 'Well, er…'

'Boyfriend?'

Tongue-tied by discomfiture, Gwenna shook her head and wished she found it easier to tell lies. 'No, but…' Her full, soft mouth folding, she dipped her head and fell silent.

She had turned down the only excuse that Angelo could have accepted. Even then he would only have sought another angle of approach, for he had yet to meet a woman capable of resisting what he offered. Fidelity, he had long since discovered, was usually negotiable. The silence lingered. He could not credit that, for the very first time in his life, he was meeting with a flat refusal.

'Excuse me,' she muttered again, her eagerness to be gone yet another rebuff to the male watching her. 'I have to go.'

Angelo stood in mute disbelief as she walked away from him and through the church gate. His gaze tracked her every move as he had a perverse need to know if she would look back; she did not.

Breathless and taut, Gwenna secured the dog lead to the wooden bench that sat to one side of the arched wooden door and stepped gratefully into the cool dim interior of the old church. Freddy and Jake chattered while she set about her task of arranging the flowers for the christening that was to take place the following morning.

It was quite some time since anyone had asked her out; she met very few fresh faces. She could not understand why she was so flustered. Or why she had the most peculiar desire to creep back to the door to peer out and see if the handsome stranger was still there, which of course he wouldn't be. He would now be well on the way to his incredibly posh hotel, which was probably hosting an international business conference or some such thing. There had been a slight inflection on certain words that had suggested that English might not be his first language. Certainly men with that kind of gloss and sophistication were scarcer than hen's teeth, locally.

What was the matter with her? Why was she even curious? She dashed impatient fingers through the strands of fair hair clinging to her damp brow. She didn't date. There was just no point when it couldn't go anywhere. She had learned the hard way that even when men said friendship was fine, they always wanted more and more always involved sex. But she didn't want physical intimacy without love, which would leave her feeling just as empty and alone when it was over. The taunts she had endured as she grew up had convinced her that old-fashioned values could provide a bulwark of protection from the worst mistakes. She was painfully aware that her own mother had paid a high price for flouting those same principles.

An image of the stranger's lean bronzed face swam before Gwenna afresh, and the extraordinary impact of those dark deep set eyes against the fantastic symmetry of his hard bone structure. A soft gurgle of laughter was reluctantly dragged from her. So, she was female and human and she had noticed a breathtakingly gorgeous guy. Not her type though. He had been altogether too arrogant and slick to appeal to her. She liked open, friendly men with a creative bent. Add in tobacco brown hair and laughing green eyes, she reflected abstractedly, and she would be describing her likeness of the perfect man.

Fifty breathless minutes later, Gwenna returned Freddy and Jake to their mother, who had had a pre-natal appointment to attend at the hospital. She knew Joyce Miller well for the two women had worked together at the nursery for over a year.

'Come in for a while,' the heavily pregnant redhead urged. 'I'll make you a cup of tea.'

'Sorry, I can't.'

Joyce gave her a wry appraisal. 'Is the Evil Witch jerking your chain again?'

Gwenna shrugged acceptance. 'There's still a few things needing done at my father's house—'

'But you don't even live there. I can't see what the state of the Old Rectory has got to do with you.'

It was quite a few years since Gwenna had moved into the small flat above the office at the nursery. Her accommodation was spartan but it had been a relief to embrace peace and independence. 'I don't mind if it keeps Eva happy. Tomorrow is a special day for Dad.'

'And for you,' Joyce chipped in. 'Masscy Manor was built by your ancestors. It was once your mother's home—'

Gwenna laughed and shook her head. 'More than a generation back and even then it was going to rack and ruin. My grandmother moved out because the roof was leaking so badly and by then she and my mother were only living in a couple of rooms. It's a pity that none of my Massey ancestors had the magic knack of making money.'

'Well, I think you've done incredibly well getting the locals together and coming up with so many good ideas to raise cash for the garden restoration.'

Gwenna grinned. 'Thanks, but I've only ever been the backroom girl. It was my father's persuasive tongue and his fantastic business connections which brought in the serious pledges of money. He's done a marvellous job. Without his input we would never have made it this far.'

'I've finally realised why you're still single. You adore your father,' the redhead said ruefully. 'No man will ever match him in your eyes.'

Walking over to the Old Rectory where her father and step-mother lived, Gwenna thought about that conversation. She had not argued the point because the truth was too private. But, even so, Gwenna did believe that for any man to match Donald Hamilton would be a very tall order indeed. Her father *was* special. It had taken an exceptional man to acknowledge an illegitimate daughter, take her into his home and keep her there even when it had cost him his marriage. She accepted that her father had his flaws. As a younger man, he had had a pronounced weakness for women and more than one extra-marital affair. Her mother, Isabel Massey, had been one of those women.

The following morning, Gwenna watched while her father posed for the cameras at the neglected main entrance of the Massey estate. Although comfortably into his fifties, Donald Hamilton looked younger. With his silvering blond hair swept back from his tanned brow, he was a very presentable man. A lawyer, who had forged a successful career with a furniture company, he was accustomed to dealing with the media and his short witty speech added gloss to an already polished public performance. The gates were swept open and the local television news team recorded the moment and punctuated it with an interview. Gwenna's stepmother and her stepsisters, Penelope and Wanda, were revelling in the limelight. Gwenna made no attempt to join the family gathering since she was well aware that she would be unwelcome and that the subsequent unpleasantness would discomfit her father.

'I didn't realise the police bigwigs were coming too,' a member of the Massey Garden committee remarked at her elbow. 'That's Chief Superintendent Clarke.'

Gwenna glanced over her shoulder and saw two men in suits standing by a police car. Their faces were grave. Another man was in conversation with her father and whatever was being said was evidently not to Donald Hamilton's liking, for he had turned a dull red and he was saying loudly that something was nonsense. The news crew were now paying attention to the tableau. With an exasperated smile on his lips, her father strode towards the men by the car, even making a laughing sally as he approached. But a curious little puddle of silence was steadily spreading through the crowd. It enabled Gwenna to hear the senior police officer refer to 'very serious allegations'. She watched in frank disbelief as her father had his legal rights read to him. In full view of his family and the media, Donald Hamilton was being arrested.

In his opulent private suite at the Peveril House hotel later that afternoon, Angelo Riccardi flicked on the recording that had been made for his benefit. Having received an anonymous tip off, the television crew had lingered for the more exciting finale that had been promised: Hamilton, captured on film at the very height of his self-glorification as local philanthropist, brought crashing down from his little plastic pedestal of respectability.

Angelo had bought the furniture company that employed his quarry and had sent in his auditors to check the accounts.

Catching Hamilton red-handed had not been the challenge he had expected. Indeed it had been almost too easy. Of course, public exposure was only the beginning, Angelo reflected. Hamilton had to be made to pay the proper price for his sins. Piece by piece he intended to strip the man who had abandoned his mother of everything he valued and his good name was only the first step in that process...

CHAPTER TWO

GWENNA looked round the noisy room in despair and blocked out the angry flood of accusations being hurled at the hunched and pathetic figure of her father, who had been shorn of all his natural buoyancy by the events of recent days.

The drawing room of the Old Rectory was large and elegant. But the flower arrangement on the table, which Gwenna had taken such special pains with, was now wilting and dropping petals. It was three days since the world in which she lived had shattered into broken shards and, along with it, some of her most heartfelt convictions.

Donald Hamilton had been charged with fraud, false accounting and forgery and informed that other offences might yet be added to that terrifying tally. At first, everybody had been up in arms in defence of the older man. Not just his family, but his friends and neighbours as well for he was a popular figure. The fact that his employer and work colleagues stayed silent and kept their distance had been loudly condemned. But then, possibly people were worried about the security of their jobs. After all it was barely a week since Furnridge Leather had been bought by Rialto, the vast corporate business empire run by Angelo Riccardi. Possibly because of that more cosmopolitan and powerful connection, the case had attracted a great deal of unpleasant publicity.

Perhaps the biggest shock of all had occurred when Donald Hamilton, confronted with overwhelming evidence of his crimes, had chosen to confess his guilt. Gwenna had been truly devastated. When he had finally been allowed home, he had taken Gwenna into his study for a private chat. There he had confided how the extravagant lifestyle he had been leading had led to steadily mounting debts that he could no longer handle.

'I just borrowed a little one month from the Furnridge accounts to tide me over,' her parent explained heavily. 'Naturally I intended to pay it back. Unfortunately Penelope sprang her big fancy wedding on us without warning and that cost a fortune. Her mother spent another fortune comforting her when her marriage failed. Last year Wanda needed the capital to set up her riding school. As you know that was another disaster and I lost a lot on that venture. But I do realise that that's no excuse for stealing. You mustn't think I'm blaming anyone either—'

'I don't…I don't.' Gwenna's throat was thick with tears as she gave the older man a comforting hug. She was well aware that nothing less than the very best was ever acceptable to her stepmother and her two stepsisters and that they expected her father to provide for their every need and want.

'You see, I've never been very good at saying no to the people I love. I'm afraid that we've been living above our means for a long time but I found it impossible to deny Eva anything. I love her *so* much, Gwenna. I don't know what I'll do if she decides to divorce me over this.'

After that illuminating conversation, Gwenna was now finding it very difficult indeed to stand by listening while the rest of her father's family made him the target of their bitter recriminations. He was a solicitor, whose main source of income had been earned by his employment at Furnridge Leather. A few hours a week, he worked for a handful of private clients, most of whom were elderly and whom he had inherited from his late father's now defunct legal practice.

'They've frozen your bank accounts. My allowance hasn't been paid. How am I supposed to pay my credit card bill?' her elder stepsister, Penelope, was demanding, her pretty face contorted with fury.

Gwenna wondered what would happen if she dared to suggest that perhaps it was time that the brunette looked for a regular job. Both her stepmother's daughters still lived at home. Penelope was twenty-seven, a part-time model who treated her career like a hobby and expected her stepfather to fund the luxuries she enjoyed. Her sibling, Wanda, was two years younger and had never held down a job for longer than six weeks.

'What about the repayments on my sports car?' Wanda was demanding. 'Where am I going to get the money to keep them up?'

Eva Hamilton gave her silent husband a bitter look of tearful condemnation. 'Until now, I never appreciated how lucky I was that my first husband was such an excellent provider.'

Gwenna winced at a reminder that she felt was unnecessarily cruel and wondered fearfully if her stepmother would stand by her disgraced husband, now that the gravy train had ground to a halt.

'Yes, he was and I'm certainly not living up to that challenge.' Slumped in his armchair in the corner, Donald Hamilton was sunk so deep in depression that he was a soft target for all such attacks.

'If only you hadn't admitted that you took the money! With a good lawyer, we could have fought the charges!' Penelope told him furiously.

'We might have had a chance if Furnridge had still been under John Ridge's ownership. But not now…Rialto is *huge* and Angelo Riccardi is a hard-hitter. In an organisation of that size, the rules are rigid and the resources unlimited. They'd pursue you to the edge of the grave for a penny, never mind what I've creamed off the accounts over the years,' the older man framed bleakly. 'I'm ruined.'

'What matters is that you owned up to what you had done. I'm sure that that was a relief to everyone concerned and that you feel a little better now,' Gwenna commented hastily.

'Honesty is the best policy? Did you get taught that in Sunday School?' Her stepmother sobbed with scorn. 'You definitely didn't pick it up at your mother's knee. After all, she was your father's secret bit on the side for years!'

Gwenna reddened with the old sense of shame that she had never managed to shake off. It was true: her mother's long-running affair with Donald Hamilton had been furtive and built on lies and pretences. Even so, while she had often been treated to such sneering reminders as a child, few had come her way since she had attained adult independence. 'Look, I came over to—'

'Stick your nose in where it's not wanted?' Wanda sniped.

'So that we could all try to work out how best to deal with this situation,' Gwenna countered doggedly. 'If we can pay back the money that's been taken, Dad might still be able to escape prosecution. Obviously the Massey gardens and the nursery could be sold. Then there's the apartment in London—'

The very suggestion that the city apartment, much used by Eva and her daughters, should be put on the market roused

Gwenna's step relatives to a vitriolic counter attack. But Donald Hamilton studied his only child with the first glimmer of hope he had displayed since his arrest. 'Do you think an offer like that could make a difference?'

Gwenna gave a vigorous nod.

'But if Massey is sold you'll lose your job, the business you've built up and the roof over your head. Would you really do that for me?' he prompted wonderingly.

'Of course.' Gwenna cleared her throat awkwardly. 'Then there's this place…'

Eva emerged from her handkerchief like a ferret scenting a rabbit. 'This house is in my name and I'm not selling it *or* raising a loan on it!'

Gwenna had not been aware of that reality and she flushed and muttered a hasty apology.

The phone rang. The police wanted her father to answer some further queries. Before Gwenna's anxious gaze the older man turned a sickly grey shade. It hurt her to witness his obvious fear at the prospect of yet another visit to the police station.

With an air of resolution, Gwenna stood up. 'I'm going to go to Furnridge Leather and ask to speak to whoever has the power to make a decision on your behalf.'

'You'll be wasting your time,' Donald mumbled. 'I'm dead in the water, dead no matter what you do.'

Angelo accepted a black coffee, but ignored the erotic invitation in the PA's admiring gaze and the manner in which she contrived to bend low enough to show off her cleavage. Where was her respect? If she had been on his personal staff she would have been history. He didn't like sex in the office. It was a distraction and he disliked distractions. Women were wonderful…outside working hours, at a convenient time of his choosing. He let nothing get in the way of business or profit.

He stood by the window that overlooked the ground-floor reception area of Furnridge Leather's premises and listened to his executives uneasily discussing ideas to regenerate the company with the former owner, John Ridge. Occasionally Angelo spoke up to rubbish the more unrealistic suggestions. This was the smallest company he had taken over in a decade. It was a challenge for his staff to think small enough to suit the project, particularly when this latest acquisition had a big black hole in its accounts. Now there were two thousand employees with very good reason to hate Donald Hamilton because the future of the business was very much in the balance.

A young woman approached the reception desk. Her long blonde hair was caught back in a simple clasp. Angelo stiffened, keen dark eyes narrowing in immediate recognition of the graceful angle of her head and her perfect profile. Well, what do you know? he thought without great surprise. Had she seen his limousine as he'd departed and recognised his financial worth? Whatever, she had evidently now identified him and intended to save him the hassle of looking for her. He felt disappointed. He had thought that just for once he might actually have to make a concentrated effort to get a woman into bed. The phone buzzed. The call was for John Ridge.

The older man set down the handset and muttered uncomfortably, 'Donald Hamilton's daughter, Gwenna, is downstairs asking to see me or whoever is in charge. Is there anyone here willing to speak to her?'

Angelo had become as still as a granite statue. He was frowning because when he had glanced through the background information on Donald Hamilton there had been no reference to a daughter by that name. 'Hamilton's *actual* daughter?'

'His only child and a lovely girl, but I would really prefer not to have to deal with her. There's nothing to say, is there?'

'Nothing,' one of the executives agreed very drily.

'I will see her in here in fifteen minutes,' Angelo decreed, rigorously suppressing the angry sense of shock and recoil spreading through him. A lovely girl? *Sì*, he could vouch for that. He was a connoisseur and she had stopped even him in his tracks. Impervious to his companions' surprise at his announcement, he immediately accessed the file on Hamilton on his laptop. And there he found the brief reference to her as Jennifer Gwendolen Massey Hamilton, aged twenty-six years. Donald Hamilton's only child, who had to be precious even to a lying, cheating fraudster.

Gwenna sat in the waiting area feeling the hostile chill in the air around her and registered that she was reaping what her father had sown. The nerve-racking minutes ticked past. She was astonished to be told that Angelo Riccardi, the billionaire head of Rialto, was in the building and prepared to speak to her, for she had dimly assumed that someone so rich and powerful would have little personal involvement in the acquisition of a comparatively small rural business. By the time she was escorted past the door that had once led to her father's office and shown into the boardroom, she was very pale, stiff with shamed discomfiture and exceedingly nervous.

'Miss Hamilton…' Angelo murmured without intonation, watching the shock of recognition stamp the pure lines of her face. She could not hide her dismay and embarrassment and he marvelled at a transparency that was a rare trait in the world in which he lived. 'I'm Angelo Riccardi.'

Astonished to be greeted by the male she had met in the village, Gwenna exclaimed in confusion, 'You're…but you can't be!'

Angelo elevated an ebony brow.

A timeless moment stretched while she stared, absorbing all over again the stunning set of his tawny gaze above the smooth dark planes of his high cheekbones, the masculine jut of his nose, the sensual fullness of his hard, handsome mouth. A curious little pulse of uneasy heat flickered in the pit of her stomach. Snatching in a ragged breath she made a mighty effort to regain her scattered wits.

'Well, obviously you are…er, who you say you are,' Gwenna conceded in an awkward rush. 'My goodness, a co-incidence I could've done without today.'

'I still don't know why you wanted to see me.' Angelo was enjoying her frank inability to conceal how flustered she was. It seemed—and he considered himself a very good judge of character—that his enemy's daughter lacked her parent's innate guile and cunning.

'To talk about my father.'

'I'm surprised you think that I would be interested.'

Gwenna stiffened. 'My father worked here for a long time—'

'While he systematically stripped this business of its capital.'

Her lashes dipped over her troubled eyes. 'I have no inten-tion of trying to deny anything that he has done.'

'Why else are you requesting this interview? But then, perhaps you expect the same special treatment that your father enjoyed when he worked here.'

Her uneasiness escalated. 'I don't know what you're talking about.'

'John Ridge treated your father more as a friend than an employee and he could never understand why improved pro-ductivity consistently failed to deliver more profits. That's why he finally sold up.' Angelo watched her lose colour and duck her head at that news. He was grimly amused by a sensitivity that he knew he would use against her. It was second nature to him to pick up on other people's weak points and utilise them for his own benefit. 'He's gutted now that he understands how his trust was betrayed.'

'Dad is very ashamed. I know that doesn't change anything—'

'You're living in your own little world, Miss Hamilton. Right now my staff are trying to find a way for this business to survive without massive redundancies.'

Her tummy executed a sick flip of alarm. Already cringing at the reminder of how John Ridge had been deceived, she was even more dismayed to learn what a precarious position the company had been left in. Angelo Riccardi's rebuke struck her as horribly well deserved; she *had* failed to consider the wider repercussions that might arise from her father's embezzlement. In fact she had naively assumed that the future of Furnridge Leather would be more secure as a part of a much larger organisation like Rialto. The risk of redundancies appalled her since the furniture company was the main local employer.

'I didn't know…I genuinely had no idea matters were so serious.'

'How could you not know? A large amount of money has been misappropriated.' Angelo was discovering that the anger roused by the disclosure of her identity had gone to be replaced by a growing buzz of satisfaction. Why not? She was Hamilton's daughter. He now had two people to play with, instead of only one, and as he was already discovering she was a very beautiful plaything with an entire repertoire of responses that he had not seen in a long time. 'No business of this size could weather such a financial loss without shedding staff.'

A gleam of optimism lightened her anxious gaze and she

lifted her head. 'But that's why I'm here…to talk about how that money could be repaid.'

'Repaid?' Angelo queried, his narrowed gaze skimming over her with renewed intensity. The upward tilt of her eyes and the sprinkling of freckles across her nose had an appeal he could not define. The trouser suit might be drab and unflattering to her frame, but it was outshone by a radiant beauty that continually drew his attention back to her.

'My father has property interests that could be sold and the proceeds put towards repayment.' Eager to put that point across, Gwenna partially evaded his gaze as she became aware of the force of his scrutiny. Not for the first time she wondered why he made her feel so uncomfortable. Her throat was tight, her muscles clenched taut. Was it fear?

'If any of those property interests were purchased with stolen funds and your father is found guilty in court, those assets could be seized and sold to provide compensation.'

That smooth assurance sliced through Gwenna's hopes like a blade and she felt the full force of her own ignorance. 'I wasn't aware of that.'

His agile intellect was already engaged in wondering what favour she had intended to ask in return for the repayment of the stolen funds. In spite of what he had said to her, he was aware that the courts were often reluctant to seize and sell private assets, particularly where there was a wife involved. It would not be the first time that a con man had served his sentence only to emerge from prison and enjoy the ill-gotten gains of his crime. That was a galling prospect to Angelo, who was determined to see Donald Hamilton punished on every possible level. Stripping the offender of his worldly goods would add savour to that process.

'However, bringing a case such as this takes time, and this

business is almost out of time.' Angelo offered up that piece of encouragement to draw her out again.

'Dad has already admitted his guilt,' Gwenna reminded him readily. 'He would be happy to agree to the properties being put up for sale and to the proceeds being used to repay his debt—'

'He's a thief, not a debtor,' Angelo cut in drily. 'What is more, although I hate to rain on your parade, property can take a very long time to sell.'

Her teeth worried anxiously at her full lower lip. Although she too had thought of that angle there was no getting round that potential hiccup that she could see. 'Yes, I appreciate that…'

Ebony eyes of extraordinary power sought and held hers in a grip as strong as forged steel. 'Of course, *if* I was prepared to consider such an arrangement, a valuation could be done and the properties concerned could simply be signed over. That could be achieved very quickly.'

Ready to grasp at any prospect of agreement, Gwenna nodded eagerly at that suggestion. She snatched in a ragged breath, wildly aware of his gaze and the insidious unsettling pulse of awareness at the secret heart of her body. Her lovely face suddenly flaming at that acknowledgement, she tore her attention from him and walked over to the window. She could not credit that *he* could have such an effect on her. He was a stranger and alien in every way to her. How could he rouse the physical consciousness that she had suppressed and buried? She refused to believe that he could. It was a long time since she had decided that she would never give her body without her heart.

'It would also lessen the risk of anyone suffering last-minute regrets,' Angelo pointed out, gaze glinting with triumph at his success in finally raising a reaction from her. He had seen the flare of surprise in her eyes. Not quite the ice maiden after all, it seemed. 'Obviously your objective is to free your father from the threat of prosecution.'

Not knowing whether to be relieved or threatened by the ease with which he had deduced that fact, Gwenna spun back to face him. She lifted her chin and knotted her hands together tightly as if she was bracing herself. 'Yes.'

'No can do, *cara*. It is my personal conviction that all wrongdoers should be punished by the full weight of the law.'

'But if that money was replaced it would benefit this business and all the people who work here!' Gwenna protested feverishly. 'Don't you care about that?'

'My heart rarely bleeds, Miss Hamilton.'

Angelo watched her brush a fine strand of honey-blonde hair back from the peach soft curve of her cheek. She was exquisite, delectable, he acknowledged, his usually disciplined body reacting with painful immediacy to the sexual charge of her presence. She was trembling almost infinitesimally. He liked the idea that he might be responsible for that potent effect. He had an almost overpowering desire to see her long hair falling loose round her shoulders in a tumbling mass of waves. That whimsical reflection surprised him but that image gave him a distinctly erotic kick.

'But in this particular case…' she dared to prompt.

'Business is all about the art of profit and the bottom line here is that there's not enough in your offer to tempt me.'

Disappointment at his refusal flooded Gwenna. She had never felt so nervous or out of her depth. At her most happy when she was working outdoors, she had acquired a host of horticultural qualifications while still regarding herself as only a keen gardener. Now, for the first time, she was uneasily conscious of her lack of sophistication. She genuinely did not know how to appeal to such a man. He had the cold, hard glitter of a very expensive and elegant diamond and he showed no emotion. It was a combination that she found utterly intimidating.

'What would it take to…er, tempt you?'

Angelo studied her with unnerving calm. 'You.'

Gwenna blinked. 'I'm sorry…I don't follow.'

'I want you.'

'I don't understand.' Her blue eyes widened and she dragged in a ragged breath. She felt incredibly stupid because of course he could not mean what she had thought he might mean. True, he had asked her out, but it had been very casual, hadn't it?

'Are you always this slow on the uptake?'

'Are you talking about…sex?' Gwenna was furious that embarrassment made her mangle that last word into an almost incomprehensible mumble.

Dense black lashes lifted over his brilliant dark tawny eyes and he managed to look very bored. 'What else?'

Gwenna surveyed him with as much unrestrained amazement as she would have shown a zebra that suddenly appeared out of nowhere to walk across the office. She had always had a problem seeing herself as a sexual being. The passes that came her way were usually pretty half-hearted because she was much better at being sympathetic and sensible than sexy. That a guy of such immense wealth and supposed sophistication should target her as if she were a provocative siren struck her as unbelievable.

'Is this some kind of a wind-up?' she asked tautly.

'I don't do wind-ups.'

Gwenna studied him, poised there so straight and tall in his sharply tailored black designer business suit. He was devastatingly handsome but she crushed that thought as soon as it entered her mind. 'But are you really suggesting that if I sleep with you you might reconsider prosecuting my father?'

'Yes.' Angelo made that confirmation.

Gwenna was stunned by that unhesitating agreement. 'But that's morally wrong.'

'We're consenting adults and you have a choice.'

Gwenna flung her head high, furious that she was dying of embarrassment like a schoolgirl, while he was behaving as though nothing untoward was happening. 'Do you get a thrill out of insulting me like this?'

'One woman's insult is another woman's compliment.' Angelo sent her a dark smile of challenge. 'It's not my ego talking, but fact, when I tell you that a score of women would kill to have the same opportunity.'

Gwenna, who rarely lost her temper, learned now that she could want to kill another human being. His insouciance, his sheer arrogance, his silken insolence, indeed the whole glossy patina of his rich and rarefied existence, which he wore like armour, made her teeth grit. Absolute hatred hurtled through her in an acrid flow. 'Well, I'm not one of them! I have higher self-esteem.'

'Which makes you infinitely more desirable.'

'So, you're one of those men who always wants most what he can't have?'

Angelo held her outraged blue gaze, more intrigued than ever by her resistance and the anger that had unexpectedly cut through her tranquil surface. 'I have never met with a "can't have",' he told her truthfully.

'You just have,' Gwenna told him grittily and turned on her heel. 'My body isn't something I'm prepared to barter, Mr Riccardi.'

'Then your father will have to pay the piper and go to prison,' Angelo murmured and she stopped halfway to the door and turned back, her raw pain at that likelihood etched in her candid gaze.

Torn between stalking out in angry mortification and the sinking conviction that she could not afford such a demonstration of disdain, Gwenna hovered. The very idea of her father going to prison appalled her. He had already lost so much: his job, his reputation, his friends, his financial security. His marriage might well soon slip into that same category of loss. She knew and she accepted that he had done wrong. But what dominated her thoughts was the debt she had owed to her father since the day that he had opened the doors of his home to her after her mother's sudden death.

When her mother, Isabel, had fallen pregnant during her long-term affair with Donald Hamilton, she'd expected her lover to leave his childless wife, Marisa. Instead Isabel had learnt that she had not been his only extra-marital interest. Heartbroken and bitter, Gwenna's mother had become a less than enthusiastic single parent.

When Gwenna was eight years old, Isabel had died in a car crash. Donald, still married to his first wife, had come to his illegitimate daughter's rescue at a time when Gwenna had had nobody else whom she could call her own. Even though he had been almost a stranger, her father had made her feel as if she truly mattered to him. Even when his long-suffering wife, Marisa, forced him to choose between his daughter and his marriage, he had refused to put Gwenna up for adoption. Not long afterwards, Marisa had demanded a divorce. The older man had never reminded Gwenna of the price he had had to pay for choosing to raise his daughter. But in spite of her father's subsequent remarriage to Eva, Gwenna had always felt very guilty. And the passage of time and the arrival of maturity had not altered her belief that she would always be in her father's debt for the loving sacrifice he had made on her behalf.

'Before you leave, hear me out,' Angelo drawled softly, playing on Gwenna's hesitation with skill and cool.

Blinking, Gwenna focused on him again.

'If sufficient assets are signed over to set against the empty coffers here at Furnridge Leather and you agree to be my mistress, I will withdraw the current charges against your father,' Angelo spelt out.

A long shiver ran through her taut, slender body. Mistress? What was that fancy term for? A one-night stand? Was conquest that important to him? Could he really want to have sex with her that much? The extent of her own sexual ignorance annoyed her.

'What does being a mistress encompass?' she pressed without looking at him.

'Pleasing me…' Angelo trailed out the word with exquisite enjoyment.

She gritted her teeth. 'I don't think I'd be very good at that.'

'I'm willing to give lessons at no extra cost.'

Furious resentment burned like lava inside her. 'I think you just can't stand being turned down…'

'I don't think you're going to turn me down twice.'

Gwenna sucked in a jerky breath. Unable even to imagine taking her clothes off in front of a man without cringing, she blanked out all thought of the nitty-gritty details of actual intimacy. She was aware that lots of people had sex without making a big issue of it. It would be physical, not emotional. There was no need for her to make a major fuss about something that really wasn't that important, she told herself urgently. She was a pragmatist. She might not be into sex but presumably she could put up with it. 'Well, as far as I'm concerned it's senseless and crazy, but if my sleeping with you one night will help my family—'

'One night won't suffice.'

Gwenna was as flattened by that unexpected comeback as if a giant rock had been dropped on her. He wanted more than one night? The silence pulsed. Newly discovered defiance made her tilt her chin. She collided with brilliant dark eyes enhanced by spiky black lashes. If eyes were truly the windows of the soul, she thought helplessly, he lacked one. 'Only hell has no time limit,' she told him prosaically.

Disconcerted by that comment, Angelo studied her and then flung back his dark head and laughed with grim appreciation. 'I like your sense of humour, *cara*.'

'But I wasn't trying to be funny. I need to know how long you envisage me filling such a strange role in your life.'

Angelo lifted a broad shoulder in a fluid shrug. But in a lightning-fast change of mood unfamiliar to him he was discovering that he had gone from amusement to an emotion very much akin to anger. He was a proud man and her parade of reluctance, which he refused to believe in, was fast becoming more insulting than intriguing. Long before they parted, she would sing a different tune, he swore inwardly. She would love him as his mother had once fruitlessly loved her con artist of a father.

'I'll want you for as long as you provide me with entertainment.'

'You find it entertaining when a woman hates you?' Gwenna asked fiercely.

Liquid gold flared in Angelo's intense gaze and it was as if all the oxygen burned up in the atmosphere between them. 'I promise you that hatred won't be what you feel.'

Gwenna compressed her generous mouth and recalled that she was supposed to feel honoured by his interest, like some maidservant of old catching the eye of the lord of the manor.

Loathing roared through her to such an extent that she felt dizzy. But then reality penetrated and she thought of her father and of how much she loved him. Angelo Riccardi was giving her the chance and the power to protect her father from prosecution and gaol. How could she say no? How many years of freedom would her father lose if she said no? How would he endure years of being shut away from the world? He would not be the same man when he emerged from such an ordeal, whereas if she kept him out of prison he would find it much easier to embark on a fresh start. What right did she have to deny him that chance of redemption?

'I want your answer now,' Angelo told her flatly.

'Yes…you've made me an offer I can't refuse,' Gwenna breathed shakily.

Angelo extended his hand.

'But let's not pretend that it's a civilised offer,' Gwenna heard herself add as she took a step back from him.

Angelo took a step forward and before she had the slightest idea of his intention he framed her cheek with long brown fingers and brought his beautiful insolent mouth down in a mocking taunt on hers. Shock held her paralysed for the first ten seconds and then a wild surge of heat flamed up between her thighs, stretching every feminine muscle wickedly taut. It was like flame in freezing temperatures, shocking and sudden and shatteringly sweet. He lifted his arrogant dark head again, his scorching dark golden gaze raking in an assessing arc over her dazed expression.

'Being civilised can be overrated, *cara*. My lawyers will be in touch. If everything is in order, I'll contact you next week.'

CHAPTER THREE

DONALD HAMILTON slowly shook his distinguished head. 'I'll have nothing left, not even my independence.'

'The valuations aren't what you hoped? Even for the city apartment?' Gwenna questioned anxiously.

'I would say that the figures are anything but generous.'

Gwenna frowned. 'Of course property prices have fallen in some areas. How did the Massey garden and nursery fare in the valuation stakes?'

'The estate is listed and protected by law,' Donald reminded her. 'That keeps its value low because there are too many rules preventing more profitable types of development. The nursery is a small enterprise. You've worked wonders there but…'

'It's hardly big business,' Gwenna filled in heavily.

'Even so, if selling up protects me from having to make a court appearance, how can I possibly complain?' her father asked her in a more upbeat tone. 'As for what you told me about you and the owner of Rialto, that's made all this even more amazing.'

Amazing? It seemed an odd choice of word. Gwenna coloured, her lashes concealing her bemused eyes. She was still wondering if the older man had quite grasped what she had delicately endeavoured to tell him with regard to her future association with Angelo Riccardi. In an effort to conceal her confusion, she bent down to pet Piglet, who was slumped at her feet.

'You're a beautiful woman and all grown up now.' Donald Hamilton treated his daughter to a distinctly misty-eyed appraisal. 'I mustn't forget that. I'm not at all surprised that a man of Angelo Riccardi's calibre should notice you and go for you in a big way.'

'Well…he did notice me,' his daughter muttered half under her breath, reckoning that her father could not possibly have registered the sort of liaison that she was being offered. No doubt that was a mercy, for she had worried about him kicking up a fuss even though she had packaged the unlovely truth with the pretence that she had been similarly impressed by Angelo Riccardi.

'Perhaps you could have a little word with him about the valuations,' the older man murmured casually. 'Not right now, necessarily, but possibly in a week or two.'

Having tensed, Gwenna slowly lifted her head. 'Have a word with him?'

'Obviously you've got influence with the man in the seat of power.'

'I don't think you can say that—'

'This is not the time for false modesty,' her father told her a touch irritably. 'Choose your moment to speak to him about how unhappy you are over the treatment of your family. My word, do I have to paint pictures for you? Have you any idea what my life is going to be like when I don't have a penny to call my own? When I'm forced to live off your stepmother like some ghastly ageing gigolo?'

But Gwenna was both taken aback and dismayed by his assumption that she would be able to persuade Angelo Riccardi to offer the older man a better price for his properties. She was very pale. 'Look, I'm sorry…I hadn't thought that far ahead yet. All I've been thinking about is keeping you out of prison.'

Donald Hamilton winced as though she had been guilty of a gross lack of tact. 'I think that risk has been safely laid to rest now and life does go on,' he declared. 'It is going to be very difficult for me to find another job.'

'Yes, I suppose it will be. But how are you expecting me to help out by speaking to Angelo Riccardi?' Gwenna asked apprehensively.

Her father grimaced. 'You can be very naïve, Gwenna. For as long as you have Riccardi's interest the world will be your oyster. Ideally I would like my job back at Furnridge Leather.'

Gwenna was staggered by that announcement. 'Your old job?'

'Yes.' Impervious to her incredulity, Donald Hamilton added, 'That would silence the scandalmongers. And help me get back on my feet again.'

Gwenna swallowed hard. 'I honestly don't think that I could do anything to help you to get your old job back.'

'Well, if not it, something of equivalent status elsewhere. Why so shocked?' he queried with dissatisfaction. 'It would be no big deal to Riccardi to do one little favour for you.'

For once, Gwenna found it a relief to be joined by Eva and her stepsisters. She did not know how to tell her father that she did not have the influence he imagined, but she did feel that his expectations were unrealistic. At the same time, she strove to make allowances for his state of mind. He was under enormous pressure and the troubled state of his relationship with his wife was not helping.

'Nice to see that you're still running round in your dreary old Barbour and jeans like Little Miss Ordinary.' Penelope treated Gwenna to a sour appraisal. 'When does Angelo Riccardi wave his magic wand and turn you into a sex kitten? Or does mud turn him on?'

Gwenna had no wish to consider what might turn Angelo Riccardi on. Ever since that startling kiss, she had blanked him out of her mind. The discovery that he could dredge such a physical response from her had been deeply unwelcome. Indeed she was mortified to her core to appreciate that she was not impervious to his sexual charge. But, equally, forewarned was forearmed, and she had no plans to gratify his ego in that manner again.

Wanda groaned with unhidden envy. 'When I think of the effort I make to look beautiful, it's depressing that you can go out looking like a dog's dinner and still pull a billionaire.'

'It won't last five minutes,' her stepmother, Eva, forecast with a dismissive but speaking distaste that raised goose bumps of chagrin below Gwenna's skin. 'These things never do.'

'I'd better go. I've got orders to take to the post office,' Gwenna muttered, keen to make her escape from the trio of cold, critical gazes fixed to her. Her stepmother's contempt bit deepest of all.

'Don't forget what I'm going through here,' her father urged, having taken the unusual step of accompanying his daughter to the door.

'Of course, I won't.' Gwenna was touched by the affectionate hug he gave her.

'See if you can work out something on my behalf with Riccardi.'

Gwenna drove slowly back to the nursery in the van. There was nothing more that she could do for her father at present, she thought unhappily. He was going to have to deal with the fact that his life was never going to be the same again, but that would take time. Her brow was pounding out her tension. Reasoning was a challenge when she felt as though the shock of recent events had set up a barrier between her and her wits. She was still struggling to accept that, in the space of ten days, her whole life had fallen down round her like a house of cards and with it the future that she had taken for granted. The village where she had lived from birth would no longer be her home. She would be barred from the gardens where she had grown up and happily worked whenever she had a moment free. The business she had laboured so hard to build would pass on to a stranger and might not even survive. After all, the profit margins at the nursery were low and, with Joyce on maternity leave, she was working alone.

Her mobile phone rang just as she finished packing the orders from the mail-order catalogue in the rear storeroom. It was Toby. Smiling with pleasure, she relaxed and went into the shop to chat and savour every piece of his news. He told her that he was in Germany. A landscape architect, Toby James had already made his name in design and he often accepted commissions abroad. Gwenna had first met him at college and saw a lot less of him than she would have liked.

'A mate of a mate saw the story about your father in the paper and passed it on,' Toby volunteered. 'You must be really torn up about this. Why didn't you tell me about it yourself?'

Piglet had started barking in the storeroom and she called out to him to hush. 'There was no point spreading the bad news.'

'How often have I cried on your shoulder?' he censured.

'Only once,' she sighed, recalling that night with pained regret. 'The nursery and the gardens are being sold.'

'That is a total disaster… I can't believe it!'

Gwenna pictured Toby raking an impatient hand through his brown hair, his green eyes glinting with concern and disappointment on her behalf. He was very attractive and tremendous fun. They had so much in common and she even got on like a house on fire with his family. It had taken a long time for her to register that their close friendship was destined to go no further because, although few people appreciated the fact, Toby was gay. By the time she'd found out she had been head over heels in love with him and had yet to meet the man who could compete with Toby's hold on her affections, although goodness knew she had tried.

While Gwenna was enjoying her conversation with Toby, Angelo was descending from his limo that had purred to a halt outside. He surveyed his surroundings with huge disdain. The nursery as such was composed of ramshackle sheds and an ancient greenhouse. He strolled towards the open door of the shop and just as he began to frown at the strong perfume in the air he saw Gwenna. Endless long slim legs clad in slim-fit jeans, blonde hair in a pony-tail, she was leaning back against the counter, a glorious smile lighting up her lovely face. She was chattering, unaware of his presence. Instantly he knew that he would not be satisfied until she smiled at him like that.

'It feels like a hundred years ago since I saw you…I miss you.'

Stilling in the doorway, Angelo began to listen. He was fifteen feet from her and she still hadn't noticed him. That had never happened to him before. The average woman went on hyper-alert when he entered the building, never mind the same room. She was locked onto that phone as if it were her lover. Or, as if she were talking to her lover, eyes shining, voice husky, giggly, her entire manner in feminine flirt mode. His eyes turned to chips of black ice.

'Things are kind of up in the air right now,' Gwenna

confided, having told Toby only what she deemed necessary for him to know, which was not a lot. 'We'll catch up when you get back.'

Gwenna did not know what it was that made her look up and when she did she jerked and almost dropped the phone. Shock gripped her vocal cords and her lungs. Angelo Riccardi was standing in the doorway, a long black cashmere overcoat hanging loose over his dark pinstripe suit, strikingly elegant, even more strikingly handsome.

'Toby…I have to go…someone's come into the shop,' Gwenna announced in a clumsy staccato rush of unease, eyes wide and defensive. Her smile had fallen off her lips as if she had been slapped.

Angelo strolled in. 'Who's Toby?' he enquired lazily.

'A friend.' Gwenna crammed the phone back in her pocket. 'How can I help you?'

'Are you going to ask me that in bed?' Angelo murmured. 'I'm not a customer.'

Hot pink washed her cheeks and only slowly receded. Her bright blue eyes touched on his and fled again, her hands clenching because he'd had the cruelty to mention what she had steadfastly refused to think about. She applied her tried-and-tested least-said-soonest-mended formula to her thoughts. As a young child she had learned the futility of excessive anticipation and worry when she was powerless to alter things. Now a tiny pulse beat out her extreme tension in the blue-veined hollow beneath her collar-bone. Even without looking at him, she felt the high-octane hum of energy that laced the atmosphere around him. It put her entire body into a crazy state of anticipation: her muscles were rigid, her breathing audible and her breasts felt heavy.

'I'd like you to show me around the estate,' Angelo imparted.

'There's not much of an estate left.'

'Whatever. I need fresh air. I can hardly breathe for the perfume in here.' Before he stepped outside, Angelo directed a cutting glance in the direction of the headily scented bowls of rosebuds and other mixtures set out by the counter.

'I make pot-pourri. It's a big seller. My customers come from miles away to buy from me,' Gwenna told him.

Angelo said nothing. With difficulty she silenced the self-protective words on her tongue. His uninterest was blatant but she reminded herself that she owed it to the Massey Garden committee to check out his intentions in advance of the takeover. She let Piglet out of the storeroom. The little dog headed for Angelo, hovered in unsuccessful hope of an ac-knowledgement, and then raced out in a delighted fury of barking to investigate the strangers outside. The parking area out front was, at first glance, packed with cars and men.

'Who are all these people?' Gwenna frowned.

'Security.'

Gwenna was tempted to make a tart comment, relating to his undoubted need to take such precautions. His brilliant tawny scrutiny met hers. 'Much better not,' he said softly. 'It's never a good idea to put me in a bad mood.'

Momentarily she shut her eyes, disconcerted by the speed with which he had read her and almost equally shaken by her ongoing need to fight with him. On the other hand the idea of giving way to the chill of fear that he evoked scared her even more. 'Only a tiny part of the gardens has been restored. I use part of the old kitchen garden to display the plants I grow in their natural habitat—'

'I wouldn't have said that this was your natural habitat.'

'Well, then, you'd be wrong—'

'I'm very rarely wrong about anything.'

Gwenna hung onto her temper with difficulty. He had come to a halt and he cast a long dark shadow.

In silence, Angelo reached for her hand and she had to combat a strong urge to whip it out of reach. Long brown fingers encircled her wrist with complete cool and exposed the roughened skin on her palms and the ragged state of her nails. 'When I realised that you ran the nursery, I didn't appreciate that that entailed working the ground like a navvy.'

Off-balanced by that physical contact, Gwenna breathed unevenly. 'That's what I enjoy the most.'

'You've led a restricted life.'

'I don't think so.'

'You're very stubborn.' Stunning dark eyes linked with hers and her chest went tight round the quickened pound of her heartbeat, until she was aware of nothing but him. He carried her fingers to his handsome mouth and pressed his lips softly to them in an elegant gesture that had immense style and assurance. 'I like it. In a world of yes-women, you shine like a star, *gioia*.'

Shivering, she jerked her hand back but she could still feel the touch of his lips on her skin like a fiery brand of intent. A hard, tight knot of heat sat low in her tummy. Nothing fazed him. His ruthlessness was like a steel wall of chain-mail. That she knew it and was *still* capable of responding to him with excitement shamed her to the core. Excitement? He'd kissed her hand and the sizzle in the air blew her mind. What did that say about her? That she had spent too long dreaming about a man she could never have? She forced a breath into her straining lungs and started talking fast about the garden and the restoration plans and funds that were already in place.

Angelo listened without interest or comment. He had no intention of agreeing commitment to a project that on the face of it offered no useful advantage or prospect of profit. He wasn't into green spaces. He had never had the time or patience to stand still and smell the roses or admire a view. Her love and enthusiasm for the hilly overgrown acres surrounding them were patent. But his mind was occupied with less innocent pleasures. He was wondering how she could look so marvellous when she was dressed like a tramp. He was keen to see her all packaged and groomed to her feminine best for his benefit. He was recalling the faint evocative perfume he had smelled on her skin, suspecting that it might possibly be the unspoilt aroma of simple soap. He was constantly noticing and being irritated by the skittish way she backed off on her long coltish legs every time he got within two feet of her.

'Stop that.'

'Stop what?' she exclaimed.

Angelo closed a restraining hand over hers and anchored her to his side.

'Mr Riccardi…'

And that formal mode of address filled him with such ferocious dissatisfaction that he hauled her to him and kissed her luscious pink lips with all the fierce desire that he usually kept in iron-clad restraint.

A muffled gasp escaped her before the descent of his hard, hungry mouth silenced her. He stole her words, her breath, her ability to think and her legs threatened to buckle under her with the shock of it. The shattering swell of excitement snatched her up into a maelstrom. The sensual thrust of his tongue into the damp interior of her mouth set her body alight with reckless response. He backed her up against the old stone wall behind her. Firm hands cupped her denim-clad buttocks, lifting her off her feet. Seductive sensation made her tingle all over. His passion was raw and thrilling and terrifyingly new to her.

Suddenly, Angelo lifted his dark head and vented what sounded like an Italian expletive. 'Your dog's bitten me…'

Momentarily speechless, Gwenna blinked and focused with difficulty on the sight of Piglet growling like mad and hauling frantically at the hem of Angelo's immaculate trousers. 'Oh, my word, he really doesn't like you…' Crouching down, trembling all over like a wobbly jelly inside and out, she was grateful for the excuse to lift the little dog up in her arms.

'*Inferno*! Is that it? No, "Are you hurt? Bleeding? In need of a tetanus shot?"' Angelo Riccardi drawled with icy sarcasm.

'I'm really sorry…are you okay?'

'I don't think I'll bleed to death. And the shots are up to date,' Angelo said very drily, unable to avoid noticing how the dog was being gently petted and soothed. He could have sworn there was a triumphant smirk in those little round doggy eyes. The fever in his blood had made him act without thinking and that awareness angered him. What was it about her? He looked forward to the aftermath of total conquest when he would no longer want her.

Legs feeling shaky, Gwenna thanked heaven for her pet's opportune intervention and moved away. Putting Piglet back onto his four stubby legs, Gwenna straightened with reluctance. She was seriously ashamed of her own behaviour and not enough of a hypocrite to tell off her pet. Not when she was convinced that Piglet had saved her from losing her virginity. She did not believe that Angelo Riccardi would have called a decent halt. He did what he liked when he liked. He had hauled her into his arms like a Viking on the rampage. He was violently oversexed. Those daunting truths had sunk in on her. Her mouth felt hot and swollen and she was afraid to look at him. 'The gardens are a wasteland beyond the wall. There's really not anything more to show you.'

'The ancestral mansion?'

A few minutes later she came to a halt a hundred yards from the large shell of the Regency house where her mother had been born. Its ruinous state had embittered Isabel Massey, who had never got over the conviction that fate had dealt her a very poor hand. In comparison, Gwenna regarded that part of her family's history with rueful acceptance, for the truth was that her Massey ancestors had been hopeless social climbers who had never been able to afford to maintain the white elephant they had built.

'What's the inside like?'

'A wreck. It had to be boarded up years ago for safety.'

'This is only a flying visit,' Angelo murmured on the walk back to the nursery. 'I should mention that your father has been called to a meeting this afternoon.'

Gwenna tensed. 'Am I allowed to ask what the meeting is about?'

'The fact that he hasn't given a truthful account of his property holdings.'

Her cheeks flamed, surprise and anger assailing her. 'That's an out-and-out lie!'

Angelo regarded her with impassive cool. 'I don't like people who waste my time.'

'But Dad hasn't been wasting your time and he hasn't lied to you either!' Her china-blue eyes sparking, Gwenna curled her hands into protective fists by her side. 'You can't assume he's deceived you just because he made the mistake of helping himself to cash at Furnridge Leather.'

'I'm not. Your father was told that he had to make a full disclosure of his assets.'

'And he has done so.'

'While carefully omitting details of the *other* London apartment he owns.'

'He only has one, for goodness' sake!'

'He's fortunate to own a second, as there is still a shortfall in the amount he has to repay.'

Gwenna sucked in a steadying breath. 'You've got it wrong.'

'I'm afraid not. My information about the second town property is from an impeccable source.' Angelo watched the fraught look of sudden uncertainty and dismay tauten her fine bone structure. She could not hide her sorrow. He could have told her that her loyalty and affection were wasted on so undeserving a cause. Donald Hamilton had an unbroken record of lying, cheating and robbing those foolish enough to place their trust in him.

Worrying at her lower lip, Gwenna turned her head away because her eyes were stinging with tears. Like it or not, there was something horribly convincing about Angelo's supreme confidence. 'If you're right, I really don't know what to say.'

'Our deal will still stand. Your father will sign over the agreed assets and we will draw a line below this matter.'

Gwenna swallowed convulsively. 'In the circumstances that's very generous of you.'

Angelo smiled. His smile would have chilled an iceberg. Events were moving exactly to plan. He was well aware that Donald Hamilton had committed at least one other offence, which would eventually surface. When it did, a court case and a custodial sentence would be a virtual certainty. By the time Angelo had finished, his quarry would have lost everything he valued.

'My father is not a bad man, just a foolish one. I don't know what's got into him…maybe it's some kind of mid-life crisis,' Gwenna reasoned in desperation. 'I honestly can't explain why he's done what he's done, or why he seems to be acting like his own worst enemy right now. But I can tell you that he's been an absolutely marvellous father to me. He's done so much work in the community as well.'

Angelo found himself focusing on the sincere glow of conviction in her damp eyes. She was like a distress beacon radiating emotion. She was not putting on a show for his benefit. He was fascinated by the feelings she could not hide. His bed partners always had a hard glossy shell that matched his renowned self-containment. Full of ideals and optimism as she was, she was ridiculously vulnerable. In a few months' time, possibly even sooner, she would be sadder and wiser. A faint stab of regret assailed him that that should be the case. Perturbed by that unwelcome jab of seeming sensitivity, he crushed it dead.

'I've organised accommodation for you.' Angelo turned to a subject of greater interest to him.

Gwenna froze, silky brown lashes screening her gaze to conceal her reaction to the sudden impact of that announcement. 'What sort of accommodation?'

'A penthouse in London…I like lofty spaces.'

'I don't…is there a garden? Piglet will need a garden,' Gwenna told him tightly.

'Piglet?' Angelo queried.

'My dog.'

'I'll pick up the bill for his stay in a pet hotel,' Angelo imparted in a dry tone of dismissal.

'No. He has to stay with me. He pines and refuses to eat when I'm not around,' Gwenna responded with unhidden anxiety. 'I know it might sound silly to someone who's not sentimental about pets…but he's a very emotional dog.'

Angelo settled his black gaze on the ugly little dog messily digging up the border behind her back. The dog with a foolish owner twisted round its short but crooked tail. No way was he prepared to share house-room even briefly with her pet. 'He goes to the hotel. My staff will choose the very best available.'

'Do I have any say about anything?' she enquired flatly.

Angelo thought hard about that. If he had had a chain attached to her ankle, he would have been set on removing links to restrict her freedom even more. It was an unfamiliar attitude to a male accustomed to easy conquest and it annoyed him. 'Your accommodation?'

Gwenna went for that assurance at speed because she saw no reason why she should be anything other than difficult. After all, she was in no hurry to fulfil the agreement he had enforced. 'I want to live somewhere with a garden,' she told him with complete truth. 'I'll go mad if I'm in the city and shut in between four walls.'

'There's a pool with a roof that rolls back.'

'I want a garden...even a condemned man gets one last request.'

'You're not facing a firing squad.' Angelo treated her to a fulminating appraisal. A garden? What the hell did she want with a garden? That was not a reasonable request. That would take more time to organise and waiting for her was killing him by inches. Ever since he had first seen her, a parade of disturbingly erotic images had kept up a constant assault on his concentration. He was tired of that mental invasion and unlikely ever to be a convert to the art of patience.

'How soon will you come to me?' Angelo prompted levelly.

Unnerved by that bold question, Gwenna made the mistake of looking directly at him. She clashed with stunning tawny eyes hot with hunger and her face flamed at what he let her see there. Her entire skin surface prickled and tightened over her bones.

'Don't pretend you don't know what I mean.' A rougher edge had entered his dark-timbred drawl.

'When I have to…when I have no choice.'

'The answer of a pure and virtuous virgin facing ravishment about a century ago.' His cynical smile of insolent amusement made the blood burn hotter than ever in her cheeks. 'Take a reality check. You're not in that category.'

'You think you know everything, don't you?' Furious resentment raced through Gwenna. 'But you don't. For what it's worth, I *am* in that category!'

His hard gaze narrowed, black spiky lashes lowering to intensify the black glitter of his potent scrutiny. He studied her in the charged silence and she dragged her attention from him, ferocious embarrassment and anger engulfing her.

Angelo was travelling from stunned surprise over her claim to a powerful surge of satisfaction. Was this the source of her unusually strong attraction for him? Had he somehow sensed the subtle distinction between her and the other women he had known? She *was* different, the exact opposite of his usual sexually adept partners. A virgin. Asking her to go back to London with him for a couple of hours to fill in the time before his flight to New York now struck him as very inappropriate, even tacky. For a split second the entire scenario felt tacky, but when he looked at her he blocked out that thought before it could get a toehold. He had never felt such an urgent desire for a woman and now that he understood that the source of her reluctance was inexperience the need to possess her had an even sharper edge. She was not indifferent or impervious to him. She was just shy, and he was willing to admit that he wasn't used to shy women.

The silence had settled like a blanket. His lack of comment suddenly infuriated her and made her feel foolish. She so wished that she had not blurted out one of her biggest secrets. 'Look, I have loads of work to do,' she muttered curtly. 'When do you expect me to come to London?'

'Next week. You'll be informed of the arrangements.' Angelo withdrew a card from his pocket. 'Should you wish to talk to me…here's my private number. You'll be able to reach me no matter where I am.'

Gwenna accepted the card, unable to imagine why she would ever wish to voluntarily seek contact with him. Her troubled thoughts were fixed to a much more important issue and, finally, she took her courage into both hands and just asked outright, 'What are you planning to do with this place?'

Angelo shrugged, his expression noncommittal.

His indifference to the future of the historic gardens pierced Gwenna to the heart and sank even her lowliest expectations to rock-bottom. His lack of interest was monumental and unapologetic. He didn't do polite pretences. She reckoned that he was probably the last man alive likely to shell out cash on a venture that would struggle to survive outside the main tourist season.

Before he climbed into the limo, Angelo glanced back in her direction. She didn't return the compliment. Scooping up the muddy little dog, which was belligerently intent on barking at the nearest car, she vanished back into the shop at speed. His aggressive jaw line clenched.

CHAPTER FOUR

FOUR days later, Gwenna was in London. The morning after her arrival, she was met at her hotel by an elegant brunette in her thirties. A senior coordinator in Angelo Riccardi's employ, it had been Delphine Harper who liaised with Gwenna on the phone and orchestrated all the arrangements to be made on her behalf.

'It's my job to ensure that you enjoy a smooth transition to city life. You have a full programme of appointments today,' Delphine trilled with a polished smile that displayed her perfect white teeth to advantage. 'First on the agenda, I've organised a viewing of the property Mr Riccardi has selected for you.'

A smooth transition? Gwenna could have wept at that useful little cover-all phrase that took no account of the drastic upheaval in her once tranquil daily existence. Only now that her contentment had been wrenched from her did she appreciate just how happy she had been pottering about with plants. The same day that Angelo had visited, her father had signed over all the property he owned. Within twenty-four hours a Rialto employee had arrived to take charge of the plant nursery. The speed of that takeover had stunned Gwenna and she'd found it very hard to hand over control of the business and the gardens she loved. She'd also had to vacate her flat above the shop in a hurry; the new manager needed the accommodation and nobody had appreciated until it was too late that she actually lived there. That had forced her to move temporarily to the Old Rectory, where everyone but her father made her feel like an unwelcome interloper.

Pressed by his daughter's reference to his owning a second apartment in London, Donald Hamilton had released a heavy sigh. 'I had very good reasons for keeping that a secret. Eva would have wanted me to sell it to buy a larger family place and I wanted to keep it for our retirement. My motives weren't entirely selfish either. The current tenant is an elderly lady with a lease due for renewal. I was worried that the change of ownership would force her out.'

'But you stayed silent about it when you had promised to disclose your assets. That must've made a poor impression on the Rialto legal team,' Gwenna pointed out uncomfortably.

'If I don't look to my own interests, who else will?' her father countered without remorse. 'Of course, I'm hoping that when you get the chance, you'll do the best you can to ease our problems here.'

Recalling that conversation, Gwenna felt her stress level merely increase. Her father's airy lack of concern about his dishonesty had unnerved her. When he'd stolen from Furnridge, it had not just been a case of a man with financial worries succumbing to a moment's temptation. His problems went deeper than that. There was a weakness in her father's character, she acknowledged unhappily. That could explain the womanising streak that had caused such havoc when he was a younger man and perhaps she had been too quick to forgive and forget his history.

'We've arrived.' Delphine's bright tones cut through Gwenna's anxious reflections and shot her back to the present.

Emerging from the car, Gwenna stared in astonishment at the substantial property in front of her.

Delphine shook out keys with a pronounced air of importance and unlocked the imposing front door. 'This has to be one of the best addresses in London.'

Gwenna froze in the marble hall, gazing round in wonderment at the pillars and the elaborate staircase. Fifty questions were on the tip of her tongue. But she was too embarrassed to direct them at her companion, lest she confirm whatever mortifying suspicions the brunette already had about Gwenna's precise relationship with her fabulously wealthy employer.

'It is a very large property, and don't be misled by its age. The house enjoys air-conditioning, touch-pad electronic controls, an integrated sound system and amazing security features,' Delphine declared.

The official tour began and stretched from a basement swimming pool, gym and wine cellar right up through the floors above and a bewildering parade of vast empty rooms and high-tech bathrooms.

Delphine started to look a shade anxious at Gwenna's continuing silence. 'The mews house at the rear has staff accommodation and garaging. Now let me show you the garden, which I believe is of special interest to you. It's large and sheltered and south-facing.'

'Please excuse me for a few minutes…er, I need to call your boss.' Gwenna squeezed the words from her dry mouth and retreated into one of the lower rooms to fumble through her bag until she located the card Angelo had given her. As she punched out the number on her mobile she blinked and shook her head several times.

The minute she heard his voice she burst into speech. 'It' Gwenna. I'm sorry to disturb you.'

Angelo almost smiled and gave his PA a wave of dismissal. 'Not at all, *gioia mia*.'

'It's just you said you'd sort out accommodation, and I'm being shown this house and I don't understand. It's a stonking great enormous mansion with eight bedrooms!'

Angelo spun round in his office chair to enjoy a view of the Manhattan skyline. 'All the properties that I use must enjoy three essentials—the maximum space, privacy and security available.'

'Yes, but a house that must be worth millions is utterly insane in these circumstances unless…er… You're not planning on *moving in* with me, are you?' Gwenna gasped in an appalled tone. That was the sole explanation for such extravagant expenditure that made sense to her.

Silence hummed at the other end of the line. Angelo was gritting his even white teeth. She might have the grace of a gazelle but she also had the diplomacy of a rampaging elephant. Didn't she know *anything* about him at all? Had not even the mildest curiosity stirred her into surfing the internet or checking out the gossip pages? He didn't *do* commitment or live-in arrangements.

'Naturally, I'm not planning to move in,' he murmured with deflating cool. 'I'm sorry if that's a disappointment.'

'Oh, my goodness, no!' Gwenna asserted at a much more cheerful pitch, quite impervious to the presence of the snub she was delivering. 'We wouldn't suit each other at all. But that doesn't explain the house when we won't last five minutes together. All this trouble and expense is so unnecessary.'

Angelo's eyes flashed tawny-gold. 'Perhaps you would like me to take you to some cheap hotel that hires out rooms by the hour!'

Gwenna bit down on her ready tongue. She was shocked

to realise that she was trembling. Honesty obviously didn't pay with him, she reflected uneasily. She had made him angry and she knew that wasn't a good idea. She dared not say what she had almost said for fear of provoking him even more. But, in her opinion, the fancy trappings of a house in Chelsea would not alter the nature of the sexual transaction he had offered her and if a cheap hotel got the wretched business over with quickly she would have been the last to complain. False pride was not one of her problems.

'If it is my wish, you will live in a stonking great mansion even if it is only for five minutes. Is that understood?' Angelo enquired in a chilling tone of finality.

'Yes,' she conceded in a voice wiped clean of any expression or life.

'I have work to do. I'll see you when I get back to London.' Angelo set down the phone. He was furious with her. He had expected her to be overjoyed with the house. It had an award-winning garden. He had *personally* selected it from his property holdings. When had he ever made that much effort for a woman?

Gwenna rejoined her guide and walked out into the beautiful garden, an oasis of peace and sunlight right in the centre of a huge city. Her eyes were stinging. She was all shaken up by that conversation with Angelo. She knew that she would not make the mistake of phoning him again. As far as he was concerned she had no rights and no opinions worth hearing that did not match his own. She would not make the mistake of forgetting that in the future.

Her next port of call with Delphine was the luxury pet hotel where a booking had already been made for Piglet's benefit. The underfloor heating, miniature bed, webcam and the promise of a daily photo and bulletin about her pet made little impression on Gwenna. She explained that she would only be making occasional use of the facilities. Piglet would be exiled only when Angelo was around and, going by Delphine's encouraging comments on her employer's schedule, Angelo was much too busy to be around that often.

One week later, her eyes bright with extreme tension, Gwenna contemplated her imminent engagement at three with Angelo and its probable conclusion. A late lunch and then? Blocking out that intimidating thought-train, she studied her reflection in the vast hall mirror.

Her shift dress was white piped with black, tailored to a perfect fit and strikingly elegant. It had a famous designer label, just like all the other garments picked by the fashion consultant who had had the task of kitting Gwenna out with a fabulous new wardrobe. In truth, Gwenna barely recognised herself after her dutiful morning visit to a beauty salon. Her honey-blonde mane of waves had been straightened into a sleek glossy fall, her face expertly made up and her eyebrows ruthlessly waxed into perfect curves. She thought she bore a striking resemblance to a doll with big blue eyes and an artificially full mouth.

She had always happily gone for the natural look, choosing comfort and practicality over style. Her use of cosmetics had encompassed a touch of mascara and lipstick on special occasions. But Angelo had plunged her into the world of fashion and beauty in which her looks were all that mattered—and she was discovering that that was her equivalent of hell. She found it very hard to walk in flimsy high heels. She absolutely loathed the fake fingernails and felt hugely uncomfortable wearing white because she was convinced that she would brush against something and soil it. Even so, not a word of complaint had passed her raspberry-tinted lips; she had learned her lesson during that single voluntary phone call to Angelo Riccardi. He wasn't interested in her personal preferences or her physical comfort. All the effort and expense that was being expended on her immaculate grooming was essentially for *his* benefit.

'The car's here.' The housekeeper opened the front door and ushered Gwenna out. It was only forty-eight hours since she had moved into the house and she still felt very much like a guest staying in a top-flight hotel. Her new home had been furnished, fully equipped and staffed without any input from her.

Gwenna slid into the waiting limo. The parlous state of her nerves offended her pride. But how did Angelo Riccardi expect her to eat when she was presumably destined to provide the evening entertainment without so much as a dress rehearsal? When her phone rang she very nearly leapt a foot in the air.

It was Angelo. 'It looks as though I'm not going to make it back in time,' he informed her grimly. 'The air traffic controllers here are calling a one-day strike.'

Gwenna blinked. 'Oh, dear…'

'*Dannazione*. I'm sorry, I was very much looking forward to seeing you,' Angelo grated, striving not to yield to the suspicion that her mild response lacked any note of dissatisfaction at his news. 'I'll call when I have more information.'

Gwenna told the chauffeur to take her to Piglet's pet hotel. As they sat in the heavy lunchtime traffic she couldn't help picturing Angelo's lean, darkly handsome face, hard with impatience. His compelling image was stuck in her mind like a fixture and she couldn't push it out again. She realised that she was being torn in two by very different reactions: a sharp and shocking sense of unexpected disappointment, accompanied by a helpless sense of relief. She was startled by that stab of regret. For goodness' sake, what was the matter with her? Okay, he was incredibly gorgeous and insanely fascinating in the same dangerous way that a sleek man-eating tiger would be. But in terms of compassion and decency Angelo Riccardi was an absolute bastard. Knowing that, how could she possibly respond to him on any level?

Her phone rang again and she tensed—but it wasn't Angelo; this time it was Toby. 'I tried to catch you at home and got your stepmother instead. Digging info out of her was not easy. Since when did you move to London and get into a relationship with some guy I've never even heard of?'

Gwenna winced. 'I only moved this week…and, er, the relationship is very new.'

'Not to mention sudden and impulsive and that is most unlike you. It can only be a wild passion—and about time too!' Toby told her cheerfully. 'Look, I'm flying in tomorrow for a meeting with a new client and I'd love to see you in the evening. We could go to a club. I could do with a chill-out session.'

Gwenna beamed. 'I'd love that too. Will you be staying long?'

'No. I have to go back to Germany to tie up loose ends on the park project.'

Comforted by the prospect of seeing Toby again, Gwenna went into the pet hotel with a spring in her step. Even though they had only been parted the night before, Piglet was as ecstatic to see his mistress as she was to see him. Having persuaded him into eating, she played with him and took him out for a walk. She was grateful to have a task to devote her energies to, for her recent period of idleness had made time hang heavy on her hands. Her plan to take the little dog home with her again was disrupted when the chauffeur came inside to pass on a message he had received on the car phone: Angelo would meet her at the same exclusive restaurant for an early dinner instead. Quite unprepared for the news that Angelo had successfully evaded being delayed abroad for the rest of the day, Gwenna was cast into renewed panic…

Having moved metaphoric mountains to overcome a major hitch in his travel schedule, Angelo was still in aggressive single-minded mode, energy pumping through him in an adrenalin-charged flow. Events had conspired to keep him out of the country longer than he had hoped and his impatience to see Gwenna had a raw edge that was unfamiliar to him.

'Miss Hamilton has arrived, boss,' Franco, his chief of security, approached Angelo's table to murmur.

Angelo picked up on the note of admiration and soft ripple of comment and lifted heads that accompanied Gwenna's passage through the restaurant. At first glance, her stunning beauty held his appreciative gaze. Yet, equally quickly, he regretted the changes he saw: he had liked the luxuriant waves in her hair and the unadorned glow of her skin. The artificial polish of perfection, however, had already taken a beating. Her shiny blonde mane of hair was wind-tossed and she had a set of clearly defined muddy little dog paw-prints stamped on the front of her dress. He rose to greet her with a smile that bore little of his usual sardonic reserve.

Mesmerised by the potent dark allure of his lean bronzed face, Gwenna could not drag her attention from him. When that smile slashed his wide sensual mouth he was staggeringly handsome, indeed nothing short of breathtaking. Ten out of ten women would appreciate him at such a moment, she assured herself hurriedly. That she should notice him too was par for the course. Had Toby been in the vicinity she was convinced she would not have registered that Angelo even

existed. Her face pink with self-consciousness, she dropped
down into the chair pulled out for her occupancy.

'I didn't think you'd make it back today at all,' she confided,
noticing that the table was set well back from the other diners
to create an exclusion zone of greater privacy for their benefit.

Scorching golden eyes locked to hers and stole the very air
from her lungs. 'I wanted to be with you and when I want
something I stop at nothing to get it.'

Detaching her gaze from his, Gwenna lowered her head.
Now she felt hot all over and there was a tightness low in her
tummy at the unmistakable awareness of his meaning and the
high voltage sexual charge that he made no attempt to hide.
'Is that your recipe for success?'

'That would be too predictable for me. I choose my battles,
gioia mia.'

As champagne was poured she grasped her glass, sipped
steadily through the effervescent bubbles tickling her nose and
studied the menu with fevered determination. He began to talk
to her about Paris and she was intrigued by the discovery that
he was an unexpectedly brilliant storyteller, capable of drawing an amusing picture with a handful of words. Enthralled,
she listened and drank more than she ate; before dinner, she
had shared a bar of chocolate with Piglet. As the champagne
stole away her remaining discomfiture she was happy to let
herself be entertained.

'Are you not eating?' Angelo enquired.

'I'm not hungry.' *Except for you*, a little voice whispered
inside her head, shocking her with that instinctive message
that rebelled against everything she had believed about her
nature. But it was true: fascination had taken a powerful hold
of her and she had shut out the voice of common sense that
usually kept her feet on the ground. Even though she had sup-

pressed that initial reckless thought she still found it almost impossible to break the potent hold of his dark golden eyes. Soon she was lost in her admiration of the ebony luxuriance of his lashes, the smooth olive planes of his hard cheekbones above the blue-black roughened skin of his jaw line and the pure masculine beauty of his wide sculpted mouth. In the same way she could not resist the exhilarating zing of awareness in the atmosphere.

Every fibre of his lean, powerful body on sexual alert, Angelo thrust his plate away. Finally he had her full attention and his predatory reaction was instinctive: to take immediate advantage. He reached for her hand. 'Let's go…' he urged huskily.

'But we haven't finished,' she framed shakily.

Angelo used his strength to inexorably tug her upright. His smouldering gaze gripped hers with a sensual force that made her knees tremble. 'We haven't even begun, *bellezza mia*.'

The buzz of conversation around them died. Gwenna was conscious of the stares as Angelo escorted her out, an arm possessively close to her slim back. Her colour was high, her legs as weak as twigs. Without warning she found herself wondering if he had been with any other woman while he'd been away and a hollow sensation filled her tummy. He tucked her into the limo, got in beside her and pulled her to him. A heartbeat later the hungry driving heat of his mouth was on hers and a blaze as hot as an indoor sun was coursing through her tremulous length. It hurt not to breathe, but it would have hurt more to do without the gloriously erotic plunge of his tongue and the sweet flood of sensation he unleashed. A vital force was energising her body to a pitch of response so intense it almost hurt.

He released her lips, leaving her gasping for air and yet stricken at that loss of contact. Her bemused blue eyes focused on him again.

'You're amazing,' Angelo purred. 'I knew you would be.'

Her lashes dropped to shadow her shaken gaze. In a matter of moments he had rewritten her knowledge of herself. Her body was crying out for him and she was shocked. She wanted him. He had made her want him. Of course, a few glasses of champagne had loosened her inhibitions, she told herself defensively. But wasn't that a good thing? Angelo Riccardi had offered her the devil's bargain, and she had surrendered choice when she agreed to share his bed in return for the charges against her father being dropped. Wasn't it wiser to make the best of a bad situation rather than try to resist the inevitable? And wouldn't asking if she was currently the only woman in his life demean her? Give him the impression that she cared?

Angelo could feel her trembling and his very sensitivity to that fact annoyed him in the same way that so many things had in recent weeks. Disturbed nights when he had tossed and turned and burned for her had presumably affected his mood. The concept of deferred satisfaction was not for him. He wasn't used to waiting for a woman. But he wasn't an animal either, was he? She was a virgin and as highly strung as one of his pedigree racehorses. Gone, he could not help noticing, was the happy aura of serenity she had exuded at their first meeting. The brutal pressure he had utilised had left its mark. But why should that bother him? As Donald Hamilton's daughter, she had been raised in the cosy comfort of middle-class respectability, he reminded himself grimly. The discovery that the world could be a much more challenging place would be a character-building exercise for her.

In the hall of the Chelsea house she gave him a swift uncertain glance from eyes as blue as the china his mother had once collected. He closed a hand to hers in an imprisoning gesture. 'You haunt my dreams,' he ground out with a harsh laugh. 'You could be seriously bad for my health.'

Gwenna was feeling slightly dizzy from the champagne. Her mind was full of muzzy, disjointed thoughts, but the bitter light in his brooding dark eyes twisted something painfully inside her. Without understanding or conscious decision she lifted a hand to trace his aggressive jaw line in a soothing motion. Then startled by that extraordinary prompting, belatedly aware that he was equally surprised as questioning gold drenched the darkness of his gaze and his ebony brows pleated, she froze in confusion.

'*Per amor di Dio,*' Angelo breathed roughly, cupping her soft cheeks between long brown fingers. 'Right now I think I could die from wanting you, *mia bella.*'

He tasted her lips with a searing sweetness that sent her every barrier crashing down. She didn't want to think, she refused to think when he bent down and scooped her up into his arms as though she weighed nothing to carry her up the handsome staircase.

CHAPTER FIVE

MERE minutes later, Gwenna caught an accidental glimpse of herself in the cheval mirror in her bedroom. Dismayed, rudely recalled to reality, she stared at her hectically flushed cheeks and swollen mouth. She looked like a shameless hussy. Air cooled her spine as Angelo ran down the zip on her dress and inched it off her shoulders.

'I feel like a slut...' she gasped strickenly.

Angelo spun her round, simmering dark eyes pinned to her unhappy face. 'That's the most ridiculous thing I ever heard, *bellezza mia*,' he censured. 'I want you and you want me. What could be more natural than the desire to make love?'

A half-dozen tart retorts hovered on the edge of Gwenna's mind but she kept them there, consciously protecting herself from a pointless outburst that would only upset her more. She was having an affair, nothing more or less, she told herself squarely. Hadn't she always been a very practical person? Flights of fancy and histrionics were not for her. She would live only in the present, taking each day as it came.

Angelo smoothed her honey-blonde hair back from her troubled brow in a motion so gentle she blinked in surprise.

'I saw you and I wanted you before you even spoke. One look and that was that.'

'But that's crazy.'

'*Dio mio*, I would have moved heaven and earth to bring us to this moment,' he drawled in a driven undertone. 'Being desired to that degree should be a source of pride to you.'

Disconcerted by that statement, she blinked. 'We…we don't think the same…'

Angelo drew her to him with strong hands, a blaze of heat in his hungry gaze. 'I wouldn't want you if you were like me.'

He claimed her luscious mouth and she trembled again, made weak by the hunger he could awaken so easily. While she struggled to catch her breath he stripped off the dress and lifted her onto the bed, peeling off her shoes and, more slowly and provocatively, then her lace-topped stockings. He punctuated each and every action with the drugging demand of his lips on hers. So roused was she by this treatment that when he attempted to step back she automatically put her arms out to prevent him and stretched up to find that taunting, teasing mouth of his for herself. An earthy laugh rasped low in his throat as he toyed with her full lower lip and let his tongue plunge deep in an erotically sweet invasion that left her gasping.

Gwenna lay on the bed where he had put her, her senses singing and quivering. She watched as he cast aside his jacket and his tie in a series of easy fluid movements. Impatient tanned fingers moved to release the buttons on his shirt. The fabric edges parted to display the sleek bronzed expanse of his muscular chest and taut flat abdomen. Her tension went up another notch.

'Relax.' Registering her apprehension in the evasive flicker of her eyes, Angelo endeavoured to employ a soothing tone for the first time in his life. 'You look incredibly lovely.'

Gwenna shot him a reluctant glance. Her tension acquired an edge of panic, for suddenly it seemed unbelievable to her that she was actually about to get into a bed with a man she barely knew. 'I could really do with another drink.'

'On the cabinet, beside you.'

Gwenna, who had hoped he would have to go off and get her a drink from somewhere, looked in dismay at the bottle of champagne and the glasses sitting in readiness. Angelo strolled round the bed and uncorked the bottle. Golden liquid foamed down into a delicate flute. He extended it with reluctance. 'You really don't need liquid anaesthesia.'

Refusing to look at him and edging away, Gwenna hugged her knees with one arm while taking a very hearty gulp of champagne.

'I understand that you're nervous—'

'Don't be ridiculous,' Gwenna gritted over the edge of the flute.

'I'll make it good, *bellezza mia*,' Angelo swore softly. 'In fact I'll make the experience addictive.'

'You couldn't possibly.'

Angelo sank down on the bed with all the panache of a tiger stretching out in the sunshine. 'I think that someone's been telling you old wives' tales. It won't hurt.'

Gwenna flushed to the roots of her hair. 'What would you know about it?'

'You may be my first virgin but I have intelligence, common sense and exceptional proficiency in certain fields.' Angelo loosened her hold on the champagne flute and eased her firmly back into his arms. 'Don't let alcohol take the edge off what promises to be a very pleasurable event.'

At the instant of contact with the muscular warmth of his lean, powerful body, she shivered violently. 'You're all ego—'

'No, all confidence.' Gazing down at her with glittering dark eyes of purpose, Angelo skimmed a casually possessive hand over the pale, slim expanse of her thigh. 'Trust me. I'm not a clumsy or selfish lover.'

Little tremors rocking her from the intimate feel of his lean fingers on the taut smoothness of her thigh, Gwenna looked up at him with bemused blue eyes. *Trust me.* It should have been a laughable request. But she was making the extraordinary discovery that she was ready and willing to be convinced even if she could not understand why that should be.

Angelo kissed her and she stopped wondering and trying to think her way round unfamiliar and complicated corners. Wanton craving took over. He unclipped her bra and the cups fell away revealing smooth white delicate curves crowned by pouting pink buds. 'You're ravishing,' he groaned appreciatively.

Gwenna was catapulted from a moment of extreme shyness over her nakedness into an infinitely more shocking surge of pleasure. She shut her eyes tight at the height of it.

'Tell me that you want me,' Angelo commanded thickly, ceasing his tantalising caresses when she was utterly enslaved by her craving for that sweet, drowning pleasure.

Her dazed blue eyes struggled to focus on him.

'I have to hear you say it, *bellezza mia*,' Angelo admitted in a fierce undertone, his hot tawny-golden gaze welded expectantly to her lovely face.

There was an unbearably tight feeling of yearning low in her pelvis. She shifted up skittishly against a hair-roughened masculine thigh, absolutely desperate for his touch, controlled by instincts far stronger than she had ever imagined. 'I *can't*…'

Angelo studied her with sizzling determination. 'Tell me.'

There was not an atom of softness in that lean, darkly handsome visage and the flaming high of anticipation he had induced came as close to physical pain as any she had ever encountered. Tears of fierce shame and angry frustration washed the backs of her eyes. 'All right!' she cried, despising herself for yielding. 'I want you!'

He stole a sexy, savage kiss that lifted her lashes and he gave her a slashing smile of challenge in reward. Coming up on his knees, he dragged a pillow across the bed and eased it below her hips. 'It'll be sublime,' he swore in a roughened undertone.

Angelo kissed her and she stiffened, the fog of pleasure had seeped away she was gripped by a stark sense of shame and denial. She felt horribly emotional and tearful. How could she have let herself enjoy it? How could she have let herself down like that? Where was her pride? She was attempting to block out those disturbing thoughts when she registered that Angelo was removing her wrist-watch.

'What are you doing?' she mumbled unevenly, lying as still as a corpse under him as if to underline the fact that he was holding her entrapped.

Impervious to the hint intended, Angelo murmured lazily, 'Giving you a present, *passione mia*.'

Her smooth brow indented. 'A present?'

She lifted her hand to examine the new watch in shock and dismay. Gold, diamonds, a famous designer name. Painful early memories of similar expensive gifts surfaced. Revulsion ripped through her and she struggled with desperate fingers to take it off again but the intricate clasp defeated her. 'No, thanks, I don't want it. Look…how do you get this off?'

Angelo rested his stubborn jaw on the heel of his hand and surveyed her with deceptively sleepy tawny eyes. 'I want you to wear it—'

'What for?' Her Delft-blue eyes flashed into direct contact with his narrowed gaze for the first time and the angry distaste etched there startled him. 'So that you can kid yourself that you're really a kind, generous guy? Or so that you can belittle me by paying me in jewellery for what I just did with you? Well, I may be stuck living in your stonking great status symbol of a mansion and forced to wear the fancy clothes that you paid for but—' Gwenna had to pause just to draw breath.

'But?' Angelo encouraged, outraged that his generosity could be twisted into an insult and rejected.

'I refuse to wear jewellery you give me.'

Angelo, confounded by her behaviour and furious with her, finally released her from his weight. 'You will if it pleases me. Consider it part of the role you took on of your own accord.'

'And do I have that role all to myself?' The question flew off Gwenna's tongue before she even realised that she intended to ask it. But just as quickly she accepted that she had to know, she simply *had* to know, whether or not she was one of a crowd.

His stunning dark gaze veiled; he was a veteran at facing down awkward questions from the women in his life. 'No comment.'

Gwenna read only one meaning into that unrevealing response. And she felt as if he'd punched a hole right through her and sent the ground beneath her feet crashing away. He wasn't even willing to be faithful to her? That new knowledge was like a jagged iceberg settling in her stomach and his unapologetic attitude was a humiliating slap in the face. How much lower could he make her sink? She was appalled by his attitude.

Distaste sliced through her. 'Then, I suppose what we just did is the equivalent of a one-night stand.'

His lean bronzed face was grim as he pulled himself up against the pillows. 'I don't do those,' Angelo growled with incredulous bite.

'Perhaps I can only face thinking about this arrangement one day at a time.' Gwenna had already been stripped of virtually everything she valued. Everything he said merely heightened the frightening sense that she was no longer in control of her own life.

Suddenly all the bewildered misery and anger and hurt she had been holding back just broke free of restraint and overflowed. 'For goodness' sake, I don't even like you! You've taken my home, my garden, my very history from me and marooned me in a city where I don't belong. You've even taken Piglet!' she launched in a wild, almost incoherent surge of condemnation, scrambling out of bed to shoot into the bathroom at speed and noisily bolt the door behind her.

Angelo heard her sob and he sprang out of bed. Outrage powering him, he pulled on his boxers. So, let her cry, get it out of her system. She was overwrought. He always gave women in tears the widest possible berth.

'Gwenna…' Angelo reached the bathroom door without having taken a conscious decision to move in that direction and knocked once. 'Open this door.'

Her eyes wet, Gwenna sucked in a ragged breath and turned on the bath taps to drown him out. Womanising louse, all sweet-talk one moment, ice-cold, heartless and utterly immoral the next. How could she have just sleepwalked into becoming the mistress of such a man?

Angelo rapped on the door again. 'I want to know you're okay. And I want to know *right now*.'

Blocking him out because she had absolutely nothing left to say to him, Gwenna slid into the warm bathwater. The hint of an intimate ache between her thighs made her pale and, reaching hurriedly for the soap, she washed with helpless urgency. Tears inched down her quivering cheeks and she dashed them away with a furious hand. Why was she crying? She never, ever cried!

Angelo tried the handle one more time and then pulled on his clothes in haste. He kicked the door at the weakest point beneath the lock and it burst open, slamming back against the wall. She was in the bath, drenched blue eyes enormous with fright, honey-blonde waves of hair cloaking her and trailing in the water.

'I'm sorry if I scared you but you should have unlocked the door,' Angelo murmured with measured quietness. 'I was concerned.'

Trembling, Gwenna stared at him, absorbing the sight of his shirt hanging loose, disclosing a muscular wedge of bronzed hair-roughened chest. Shock was rippling through her. He had kicked in the door. She couldn't believe he had done that. She tipped up her chin to snatch a glance at his lean strong face and then hurriedly jerked her head away, out of breath and more tense than ever.

Angelo crouched down by the side of the bath. 'Look at me…'

'Do you have to be so intimidating?' she muttered tautly, sitting knees to chin in the water, naked and cornered.

'I'm trying hard not to be!' Angelo flared back at her. 'Stop cringing…you don't have to be afraid of me.'

Gwenna dropped her head. How could she not be afraid?

'I would never harm you.'

Gwenna thought about the kind of harm that had a more lasting effect than mere bruises.

Frustration was roaring through Angelo. She wasn't listening to him. She often gave him the impression that she was only giving him part of her attention. Not in bed though, he reminded himself with grim satisfaction. But the rest of the time? Either he got the feeling she was holding back or she was lost in her own little world and he didn't like either sensation. 'I want to understand why you blew up over the watch.'

Gwenna studied the clear water lapping round her legs and compressed her full ripe mouth. 'Dad was always giving stuff like that to my mother.'

His brows pleated. 'So? He was her husband.'

Gwenna was surprised enough to look up again. She had forgotten that he had moved down to her level and she collided unwarily with lustrous dark eyes the colour of autumn. A very dangerous man with strikingly beautiful eyes that made her heartbeat race. She shut her eyes tight in self-reproach. What was the matter with her?

'Gwenna,' Angelo chided huskily. 'I thought women loved to talk about themselves. What's wrong with you?'

'My father wasn't married to my mother,' she admitted flatly.

Angelo frowned. 'I don't follow.'

Gwenna reddened. 'Mum had an affair with Dad that dragged on for years and years. He was married to his first wife then.'

'I wasn't aware that your father had been married twice.'

'Yeah, well, why would you be?' Gwenna was mortified by the need to explain the unpalatable facts. 'When Mum fell pregnant with me she thought he would leave his wife, who couldn't have children. But he didn't. Sometimes we didn't see Dad for months on end and then he'd come visiting with extravagant pressies. My mother liked things like that...I don't.'

'But your father must've raised you...you have his name,' Angelo pointed out flatly.

'Mum died when I was eight and I went to live with Dad. His first wife wasn't happy about that and they divorced.'

'I had no idea.' Angelo was furious that the confidential

report he had had done on Hamilton had omitted such highly relevant details. He was astonished by the reality that her mother appeared to have been yet another one of the older man's sadly deluded female victims. But no sooner had that angle occurred to Angelo than he reminded himself that she was *still* Donald Hamilton's only child with the taint of his blood in her veins.

Gwenna watched him rise to his full imposing height, the sleek, hard planes of his darkly handsome features shuttered and cool. She assumed that the story she had just told him had made him think less of her. A lot of people had despised her mother for having an affair with another woman's husband and giving birth to his child. Taunted and teased at primary school, Gwenna had had few friends. The locals had expressed their scorn and disapproval by excluding Donald Hamilton's mistress and child from community activities.

In the uneasy silence, Angelo squashed the urge to ask further personal questions. He did not *do* personal in relationships. He kept it simple. He strolled out of the bathroom. *I don't even like you.* That assertion rang clear as a bell in his head all over again, infuriating him. Since when had he cared whether he was liked or not? But then women made a real effort to please him. They were deferential, flattering… *servile*? The suspicion revolted him. Couldn't he handle a challenge? Wasn't he man enough to handle what could just be the very first honest woman he had met? At the last possible moment, Angelo paused in the doorway. Tugging a fleecy towel off the rail he shook it out and strode back to extend it to her. 'Stop worrying about things.'

'I'm not worried.'

'You're stressed out of your mind,' Angelo corrected.

In an abrupt movement she scrambled up, water streaming

off her slender curves in rivulets, and accepted the embrace of the towel. She felt manipulated, controlled, managed into doing what he wanted her to do. He lifted her out of the bath.

'Don't,' she dared, drawing hurriedly back from him to firmly anchor the towel beneath her arms.

Gleaming eyes surveyed her from below a lush fringe of black lashes and she could feel her skin tightening and burning over her cheeks. Her lips felt full and moist and she imagined and immediately craved the scorching heat and pressure of his mouth on hers. She went rigid in rejection but still cruel sensation leapt and danced over her, wreaking havoc with her body. She was madly conscious and thoroughly ashamed of the straining prominence of her nipples and the wicked dampness of the tender place between her thighs.

'You see, you may not like me, *passione mia*,' Angelo murmured silkily, 'but all I have to do is carry you back to that bed and you're one hundred per cent mine.'

Gwenna was white with humiliation and self-loathing and she reacted with anger to that derisive gibe. 'I'm not yours and I never will be because you can't touch me where it matters,' she launched back furiously. 'I don't care what you think of me, or what you say or do with anyone else either, because I gave my heart a long time ago to someone worth ten of you!'

As Gwenna spun away to the vanity basin Angelo closed a lean, strong hand to a slim white shoulder to turn her back. Incredulous dark eyes flashed down at her. 'Are you saying what I think you're saying? You're telling me that you're in love with another man?' he pressed in a raw undertone.

Slowly she nodded, savouring the anger she had roused and yet disturbed by that ungenerous response. Being mean, argumentative or vengeful had not come naturally to her until she had met him. The reactions Angelo Riccardi incited were as foreign to her nature as the emotional highs and lows she was experiencing. 'I don't like the way you make me behave.'

'*You* don't like?' Angelo framed in a dark, deep voice redolent of thunder in a confined space. '*Dannazione*! Who is this guy?'

Gwenna tilted her chin. 'You don't have the right to ask me that question.'

Angelo's lean, shapely hands clenched into potent fists. He did not lose his temper. He never, ever lost it and prided himself on his rock-solid self-control. But a rage like a burning blinding surge of darkness was rising up inside him. Barely able to credit her answer, he strode into the bedroom and swung forcefully back to face her. 'On the contrary, I have every right. I set no boundaries on our arrangement.'

'You wanted my body and you've got it. You didn't ask for and you're certainly not getting anything else!' Gwenna muttered bitterly.

'His name,' Angelo framed in a tone of ice.

'None of your business.'

Angelo fixed his tie and reached for his jacket. She was hyper-aware of his every move.

'Your attitude offends me,' Angelo delivered with lethal cool.

Her fingernails dug stinging crescents into her palms. The silence was awesome and terrifying in its totality. 'Ditto.'

Angelo settled his chillingly intelligent gaze on her. 'We have an agreement and you won't walk away from it until I choose to set you free. You can't insult me into dumping you.'

'Is that what I'm doing?'

But Angelo didn't answer her. He walked out without another word. Snatching in a sustaining breath, she studied the door with the busted lock. Her legs feeling wobbly, she sank down on the bed. He had gone and, instead of being

over the moon, she felt annoyed and confused and...
strangely abandoned. Had he left to take advantage of more
entertaining and compliant female company? Her small
white teeth gritted. She hated him with a passion. She had
not thought it possible to hate anyone so much. Indeed she
had not realised that she had it in her to loathe any living
being with such venom. That he should refuse even to be
faithful was the ultimate put-down. She was glad she had
come clean and told him that she was in love with someone
else. That had offended him. How dared he talk to her as if
she *belonged* to him? How dared he? Yet when he came
close or touched her she couldn't say no to him and he knew
it. Indeed he knew his own power so well he had thrown it
in her face.

Hastily Gwenna stifled that disquieting train of thought.
Her attraction to him was a crude, coarse, hormonal thing that
had got the better of her self-discipline, she reasoned painfully. An irrational chemical reaction. Had she contrived to lie
there like a stone statue he would've been a lot less keen. She
glanced down and belatedly realised that she was still wearing
the watch and that she had actually worn it in the bath. In
guilty consternation, she examined it. The water had got in
and fogged up the face. Had he noticed? She hoped he hadn't
assumed that she had deliberately set out to damage it...

The diamond watch that swam without a lifebelt. Maybe she
would take a hammer to it next, Angelo mused, his handsome
mouth set in a bloodless line as his limo ferried him across
the city. She didn't want anything he gave her. Nor did she
appreciate anything. Not the house, the garden, the clothes,
the fabulous lifestyle that he had created for her benefit. Yet
when had he ever made so much effort? Where, one might

have wondered, was the punishment factor in his acquisition of his enemy's daughter?

Eyes hot as a bonfire, Angelo knocked back a brandy and savoured his misfortunes. Indifferent to the luxury that he offered, she preferred dressing like a tramp and grubbing through the soil in all weathers. That distance he had sensed within her? Oh, yes, there was very good reason for that distance. Although she was sleeping in *his* bed, it was in body rather than spirit because she loved another man. That struck Angelo as a deeply unnatural, distasteful and indeed outrageous state of affairs.

He was astonished at how bitter, affronted and cheated he felt. No woman had ever had that effect on him. But then no woman had ever regarded him as less than the main event. Revenge was threatening to take on a twist and rebound on him. He should ditch her, forget about her. What man would accept the role of second best in a woman's bed? Angelo wanted very badly to smash something. Maybe a whole lot of somethings. In an implacable rage he told his chauffeur to head for a nightclub. There was a hell of a lot of other women available…

The following morning, Angelo attended a board meeting. He had had very little sleep. He had got drunk the night before, something he had not done since he was a teenager. Once he had learnt that his father had had a problem with alcohol, he had been ultra careful to monitor his consumption and he was annoyed and disturbed by his lack of discipline.

Gwenna was out in the garden when Angelo called her at noon.

The dark timbre of his deep voice vibrated down her spine and her tummy clenched. Sensual imagery threatened to engulf her and she tensed as though she had been slapped. No matter how hard she policed her mind he continually forged a bold passage into her thoughts. 'Yes?' she prompted tightly.

'I'm planning to take you somewhere special tonight,' Angelo told her smoothly.

Her bright blue eyes widened in dismay. 'But I can't see you tonight—'

'Why not?'

Gwenna had no intention of cancelling her night out with Toby. 'I'm already going out. I organised it yesterday.'

'*Un*-organise it.' With difficulty Angelo haltered his temper that was on a short fuse after the events of the past twenty-four hours. 'I want to see you this evening.'

'But I can't alter the arrangement—this particular friend won't be available another time.'

'What gender is the friend?'

She stiffened. 'I don't have to answer that—'

'You just did.'

'He's a friend…okay?' Gwenna fired back, sudden guilt coming at her out of nowhere, which she fiercely fought off. How much honesty did she really owe Angelo Riccardi?

'I'll meet up with you, then. Give me a time, a place.'

She was aghast at that suggestion. 'No way! I'm sorry, but I didn't know you were planning to see me tonight. You can't expect me to be available twenty-four hours a day!'

'I do.'

'I'll start tomorrow…please be reasonable.'

Unhappily, Angelo was not in a reasonable mood. Refusal rarely came his way. Refusal in the face of his expressed displeasure had never come his way. He called Franco and instructed him to ensure that Gwenna was watched over from a discreet distance. He thought he should know where she was, what she was doing, who she was with. He did, however, have complete trust in her. After all, she had been a virgin, which suggested that the object of her affections was, for whatever reasons, unattainable. On that basis, Angelo decided that there was no reason why he should even think about the matter.

The bottom line for Angelo was that he *still* wanted Gwenna Hamilton. Even angry with her, he had fallen asleep aching for her and woken up in a worse state. He didn't like that. But the more she held back and refused to play by his rules, the more determined he became to hold onto her. Was he suffering from some knee-jerk primal reaction to the challenge she set? Whatever, he was becoming increasingly eager for the moment when cool reason would be reinstated and he would find her more tiresome than desirable.

CHAPTER SIX

'I'VE been doing some research on your boyfriend,' Toby confided with a disapproving shake of his head over drinks in a fashionable bar. 'You're seriously out of your league.'

Gwenna wrinkled her nose in reproof. 'What happened to tact?'

'Your friends are supposed to be honest. From what I can understand, Angelo Riccardi makes it a mission to live up to his bad reputation.' Toby pushed his tobacco-brown hair off his brow in a rueful gesture.

An unexpected current of irritation darting through her in response to that criticism of Angelo, Gwenna folded her lips. 'In what way?'

'In every way. He's a shark in business and he runs through women like a knife through butter. I mean, what are you playing at? You're a softy—'

'Perhaps Angelo brings out the concrete in me. I don't know why we're talking about him—'

'How about he's a billionaire? He's an urban predator and you're a country mouse? You have nothing in common with him. Of course I'm concerned about you.'

'But when I spoke to you yesterday you talked like you

approved,' Gwenna reminded him in bewilderment. 'You said
I needed passion in my life.'

'Where were you last night?'

'Why?'

Toby grimaced. 'I didn't want to be the one to tell you
but—according to the newspaper I read over my breakfast—
Angelo Riccardi was partying very publicly with three fashion
models last night.'

In shock, Gwenna went very still. So awful was the pain
she couldn't immediately speak or breathe. She wanted to
argue that Angelo had been with her the previous evening but
he had left early. In the mood he had been in, it was very
possible that he had sought out the sort of women who would
tell him how fantastic he was and swoon over a diamond
watch. Whereas she had locked herself in the bathroom, wept,
told a sad story and served him with a large bitter dollop of
home truths. No comparison, was there?

'Don't you read the newspapers?' Toby sighed.

It took effort but she made a stumbling recovery. 'Not the
sort that devote space to rumours like that.'

'I don't think it's a rumour, Gwenna.'

Gwenna struggled hard to blank out what Toby had just
told her. Why should she care? Why should the news hurt so
much? And how could she be shocked when Angelo had
slickly sidestepped an opportunity to promise fidelity? Nor
could she understand her almost overwhelming urge to track
Angelo down and confront him. Indeed the incomprehensible power of her reactions frankly appalled her.

'You're honest and loyal and you deserve better than him,'
Toby declared bracingly.

'It's not important. Do you think I don't know that Angelo
and I won't last five minutes?' Gwenna fixed a bright smile

on her mouth, but her facial muscles felt as if they were set in solid cement. 'But, hey, I'm twenty-six and I felt it was time to take a few risks.'

But the gloss went off her evening at that point and she couldn't recapture it. She loved talking to Toby and she found she would get lost in an interesting dialogue about his work, only to have enjoyment vanish when a stab of memory pierced her afresh. She couldn't really think of anything but Angelo for longer than five minutes. Her imagination kept on flashing up horribly creative pictures of Angelo playing around with a group of dazzling women. Time and time again she rearranged her thoughts.

Across London, Angelo was working late. He couldn't settle, though. He paced round his office and finally phoned Franco to find out exactly where Gwenna was. After all, she had spent the whole evening with her friend. An hour later, he strolled into the chill-out room of the same club and saw Gwenna standing with a rangy guy with floppy brown hair. Honey-blonde waves rippling down her back, she was simply dressed in jeans and a blue vest top. He was torn between satisfaction and annoyance; satisfaction that she hadn't bothered dressing up for her male companion's benefit and annoyance that she had totally ignored her vast new collection of designer clothes.

An unwilling smile playing round the edges of his handsome mouth, Angelo headed towards Gwenna and her escort. Franco was organising a table and drinks and the club manager was hovering at a respectful distance. In his readiness to play host, Angelo felt that he was being very civilised, very liberal. The dark mood that had powered him throughout the day was lifting, lightening. But as his attention lingered on Gwenna he caught the expression on her face as she glanced up at her companion. To Angelo's razor-sharp gaze the loving warmth of that look was indisputable. His lean powerful frame went rigid. It was as if something vital tore asunder inside him and savage anger flooded into the dangerous gap that opened up.

Gwenna only realised that Angelo had arrived when he closed an arm round her to say flatly, 'Time for you to say goodnight.'

She twisted round and met scorching dark eyes and her heart jumped as if someone had pushed a panic button somewhere inside her. Resentment and excitement melded into an indistinguishable whole. 'How did you know where I was?'

Angelo shifted her to one side and nodded to the older man, who was awaiting instruction nearby. 'Franco will see you out to the limo. I want a word with your...*friend* in private, *bellezza mia*.'

The deliberate hesitation in his reference to Toby made Gwenna stiffen. Mental alarm bells ringing, she picked up on the current of primitive masculine aggression Angelo exuded. Consternation gripped her but she could not quite credit her suspicions. 'Angelo, for goodness' sake—'

'Go with Franco.'

'Don't you dare touch Toby!' Gwenna gasped in a panic, hastily stepping in front of the younger man, for the dark menace in Angelo's lean, strong features was unmistakable.

A savage wave of anger gripped Angelo. That she should oppose him and put herself at risk in a ridiculous effort to protect another man only heightened his antagonism. But a glimpse of the apprehension in her expressive eyes snapped him straight back into control.

'Come home with me, then,' he breathed tautly.

'I'm not going any place with you.' Yet, Gwenna still couldn't take her eyes off Angelo. There was a light in his brilliant, brooding dark eyes that held her tighter than any chain. Slowly her attention stretched to encompass the impressive whole. In tailored black chinos worn with a striped designer shirt open at the neck, he looked absolutely gorgeous. As usual she was full of wildly conflicting responses. When she had believed he was about to thump Toby she had been terrified and then madly relieved by his withdrawal. Now her anger escalated in direct response to the fierce emotions she had been suppressing all evening.

'I'm Toby James…just by the way, in case anyone's interested in knowing that,' Toby remarked wryly, hovering and much intrigued by the proceedings.

'I'm not,' Angelo imparted without looking in his direction.

'You're just so rude…you've got no manners!' Gwenna simply exploded into speech, startling herself with that outburst as much as she startled Angelo.

'One model is infidelity, two models is greed, three is hopelessly decadent,' Toby extended in obliging explanation for Angelo's benefit.

Pale as milk, Gwenna refused to even look in Angelo's direction. 'Let's dance, Toby.'

'I think you should have this out with Angelo…only not *here* because we're attracting attention,' Toby spelt out in a suggestive whisper.

Still ignoring him, Angelo strode forward and closed a hand like a cast-iron anchor to Gwenna's narrow wrist. Long, lean fingers smoothed her delicate bones, but when she tried to pull free he retained his hold. 'We're going.'

Furious pink flushed her cheeks. Had Toby not reminded her that she was in a public place she would have screeched back at Angelo like a harpy. But she was keen to leave and say what she wanted to say with dignity. Chin at a pugnacious angle, she bade Toby goodbye and told him she'd phone him.

'Not if I've got anything to do with it,' Angelo contradicted in a raw undertone as he walked her away. 'You told me you were out with a friend. I *believed* you—'

'I was out with a friend.'

'Where did you get the idea that you could fool me?' Angelo shot her a chilling glance. 'Now I know you can't be trusted, you'll have company everywhere you go.'

'I can't believe you have the nerve to talk like this to me. You just ignored what Toby said about the models you were with last night!'

'I have nothing to say on that score,' Angelo delivered with the lethal hard-nosed cool that always silenced female pretensions.

'But I've got plenty to say,' Gwenna hissed on the pavement outside. 'No, I'm not getting into your limo. I have no need of a lift—'

Angelo shot her a warning glance from glittering dark eyes. 'I won't tolerate a scene.'

'Well, I'll keep it short and sweet.' Gwenna squared her narrow shoulders and wondered why Franco was staring at her as if she had suddenly sprouted angel wings and a halo. 'Just two little words…*it's over.*'

Sizzling gold burnished the darkness of Angelo's sceptical gaze. 'What the hell are you talking about? What's over?'

'Angelo Riccardi…you are dumped!' Gwenna launched back at him full volume. 'Do you want it in writing?'

Angelo slung her an exasperated appraisal. Espying a man with a camera moving rapidly in their direction, he scooped her up and settled her bodily into the rear seat of the limo. He slid in beside her. 'We'll discuss this in private.'

'I thought you had nothing more to say on that score!' Gwenna reminded him irately as the car moved off.

Angelo reached for her, knotting a lean brown hand into the honey-blonde luxuriance of her hair to hold her fast. Breathing in short, shallow spurts, she focused on him in surprise and a second later he claimed her luscious pink lips with ravenous driving heat. Her head swam and her body clenched tight. She quivered violently in the circle of his arms.

'I hate you,' she whispered fiercely.

Smouldering dark eyes held hers. 'So? It's far from over.'

Gwenna raked trembling fingers through her wildly tumbled hair and twisted away from him into the far corner of the seat. Shame over her surrender threatened to choke her and she fought it by keeping her next move on track. 'I haven't got time for this and we've got nothing to discuss. I have to pack and pick up Piglet.'

Angelo wanted to drag her down horizontal and finish what he had started. He was painfully aroused and hugely angry and the last thing he wanted to do was talk. He couldn't believe she was still doggedly fighting him. Men feared his anger, his power, his opposition. Women, however, loved his power, his arrogance, his strength. Why didn't she? He remembered her in the sunlight outside that church: serene and beautiful and gentle. He filed that soothing image away again. She had a core of steel, he acknowledged grimly.

Only when Gwenna stalked out of the car and into a porticoed entrance did she appreciate that she was not where she had expected to be. She rounded on Angelo. 'Whose house is this? Where have you brought me?'

'My place.' Angelo dismissed the hovering staff with a practised inclination of his handsome dark head and ensured that the front door was locked behind him. 'You're honoured. My house is a very private space.'

Refusing to be impressed by that claim or intimidated by the soaring ceiling and marble pillars, Gwenna flung her head back. 'You're wasting your breath. I refuse to have anything more to do with you!'

'And where were your standards tonight?' Angelo derided, strolling forward, which had the immediate effect of making her back away. 'You set up a meeting with the guy you love behind my back!'

The colour drained from Gwenna's face leaving her eyes looking a more vivid blue than ever against her pallor. How had he guessed? How on earth had he worked that out?

'When you agreed to be with me you never mentioned him,' Angelo continued in attack mode. 'How truthful was that?'

'I didn't think you'd be interested—'

'*Che idea!* No, that's the sort of information every man wants up front and you know it.' Glittering dark eyes slashed over her with punitive force and she quailed. 'And when you went sneaking off to see him tonight—'

'I did not sneak!' Anger surged to Gwenna's aid again.

'Yes, you did. It was much more than an innocent night out with a friend. How fair and decent was your behaviour?'

'According to some newspaper, you were out on the town with three other women last night, so what's your problem? You can't expect me to be truthful and decent when you're out cavorting with a bunch of tarts!' Gwenna shot back at him full volume.

'You're getting hysterical—'

'No, I'm giving you the truth you said you wanted and I don't think you like it much!'

'Our agreement doesn't give you the right to question my

every move or make new rules,' Angelo delivered with icy conviction.

'That's okay. I don't care.' Gwenna walked past him, a tight, hard knot in her tummy, her eyes hot and gritty with stinging tears. 'I'm not staying here one minute longer, though. No agreement is capable of forcing me to share a bed with a guy who sleeps around—'

'*Dio mio*…I don't sleep around!'

'There's no point you arguing with me. My mother may have chosen to accept a relationship of that sort—'

'*Accidenti*—do you dare to compare me to your father?' Angelo thundered in raw disbelief.

'All I'm saying is that I won't let any man make a fool of me like that. It's me and *only* me, or you can't have me at all and not all the money in the world is going to change that,' Gwenna swore shakily, her slender back ramrod-straight. But she was doubly mortified by his palpable distaste for her father. 'So, open that door and let me out.'

Angelo swore in vicious frustrated Italian.

'You virtually kidnapped me. I didn't agree to come here,' she reminded him steadfastly, only the nervous clenching and unclenching of her slim hands by her sides betraying the level of her agitation. 'Keeping me here against my will is just not on, Angelo.'

Lean, powerful face rigid, Angelo studied her with seething intensity. The silence pounded and stretched. And then he dragged in a slow deep breath and said grittily, 'Nothing happened last night.'

Gwenna studied him fixedly. A flood of relief washed over her and left her dizzy and more hopelessly confused than ever. It was not only her pride and sense of decency that had been offended by his apparent faithlessness, she registered in dismay. She had been downright tormented by the idea that he might have been with someone else. She had been jealous, hurt and furious.

Lean, angular features taut, Angelo set his perfect white teeth together. 'I didn't touch them…the models…they were company. That's all.'

'Did the company stay clothed?'

'*Sì,*' Angelo ground out as if he were being tortured, and that was very much how he felt. Why wasn't he throwing her out of his house and his life? But the closer she got to the door, the more urgent became his desire to haul her back from it. It was lust, total overpowering lust, and one taste of her had set up one very powerful craving. He loathed the very suspicion that he was no longer one hundred per cent in control, but need was overriding principle.

Gwenna realised that her legs were quaking beneath her. Slowly she turned back to face him fully. 'Okay…do you think you can do faithful now?' she asked with sincerity. 'There's no point me hanging around if you can't.'

Angelo dug potent fists of naked outrage and aggression into the pockets of his well-cut trousers. He could not believe what she was doing to him. What did it take to satisfy her? She was as persistent as water dripping on stone. Plain questions left no room for prevarication. He felt like a wild bear being chained up and forced to learn demeaning tricks. '*Per meraviglia—*'

'Just yes or no will do,' she whispered in helpful interruption.

Stubborn jaw line set at a most forbidding slant, Angelo was set on categorical resistance when he first rested his hard gaze on her. He did not respond to demands. He guarded his freedom. But with her honey-blonde curls tangled by his fingers and her pink pouting mouth slightly puffy from the imprint of his, she made a picture capable of enticing him over a cliff edge. She looked impossibly sexy. Later he did not recall the moment when he decided to surrender. '*Sì*...yes.' He closed the distance between them in two graceful strides and closed his hands over hers. 'You'll stay?'

Unprepared for the immediacy of that demand, Gwenna blinked and mumbled, 'But—'

'But nothing, *bellezza mia*. I've agreed. I've given you what you want.'

With that resolute reminder, Angelo angled her head back and drew her close before she could think up any further refinements. He let his provocative mouth glide down the extended length of her neck. A sensation like hot wires tightening sent a frisson of delicious heat darting through her pelvis and she shivered and moaned. He pushed open a door into a dimly lit room and pressed her back against the wall. The heavy pressure of his lean, hard, muscular body against hers sparked a tantalising tingle of delicious warmth. In the midst of an exchange of hot, driving kisses, she found herself pushing back against him. She squirmed against him, her fingers roving over his broad shoulders, delving into his black hair and finally forcing a path between their bodies to rip at the buttons of his shirt.

She wanted to touch him so badly she could hardly bear it and splayed her fingers across his hard, flat stomach, revelling in the feel of his warm bare skin.

'Don't do that,' Angelo groaned, pushing away her hand and lifting her into abrasive connection with his fierce erection. He crushed her full, soft lips below his and plundered the damp interior of her mouth with an explicit sensual force that left her trembling.

'Angelo—'

'Later…all that you want but not now, *cara*.'

Angelo surveyed her with rampant appreciation and dropped a teasing kiss on her brow. So what if he had never done fidelity before? He had never spared much thought for his sexual relationships, but he was becoming powerfully aware that she had an extra-special something that brought a whole new dimension to their every encounter. He should be congratulating himself on his amazing perception. Had he not recognised her extraordinary appeal the very first moment he met her? Hamilton's daughter she might be, but she was also a triumph worth a harem of ten. Smiling, he vaulted lithely upright and rearranged his clothing.

Like a sleepwalker, Gwenna scrambled up on unsteady legs, wrenching at her vest with one hand and going for her discarded jeans with the other. She was embarrassed, hopelessly unsure of how to behave. Her mind was in total turmoil. Everything she had believed she knew about herself was being turned upside down. But she fought off her misgivings and reminded herself that Angelo seemed to be making a genuine effort.

After all, hadn't he come looking for her this evening? He had been annoyed to find her with Toby. Had he been jealous? Perhaps Angelo was not quite as cold and unfeeling as his womanising reputation. Hadn't he told her that she should be proud of the fact that he wanted her so much? Maybe she was ridiculously old-fashioned. Maybe she needed to loosen up a little and stop fretting about the moralities. Although it was obvious that a promise of fidelity was a major undertaking for him, he had given it to her, she reminded herself bracingly. No longer was everything on his terms.

'We need a shower.' With that husky, mocking assurance, Angelo closed a lean hand over hers and walked her upstairs.

Gwenna was in a daze—a happy daze, and that acknowledgement stunned her. Her fingers trembled in his and his grip tightened. She had the feeling he didn't want to let go of her and she liked that. He was making her feel things she didn't understand, making her think things that struck her as unwise. It was just the impact of all the physical stuff that was confusing her, she reasoned, hurriedly squashing an almost overwhelming sense of vulnerability.

Her mobile phone rang two steps inside the door of a palatial bedroom. She dug it out to answer and walked away from Angelo the minute she recognised Toby's familiar voice. 'Yes, of course, I'm all right,' she muttered in some embarrassment.

Angelo froze, dark eyes flaring angrily as he worked out who had called her. Here she was in *his* bedroom and she was just chatting to the guy as though that was all right, acceptable, even normal. His perfect white teeth gritted when she gave him an apologetic glance and finished the conversation with the gentle assurance that she would be in touch soon. She smothered a yawn with a polite hand.

'I don't think you should be accepting calls from him.'

Delft-blue eyes met his in honest surprise. 'Why not? Toby's my oldest friend.'

'You're in love with him,' Angelo spelt out with stinging cool.

'But nothing's going to happen. Toby doesn't think of me that way.' Embarrassment and uncertainty, however, were claiming her. She always tried to be fair, always endeavoured to look at opposing points of view. It occurred to her that in the light of the fuss she had made about fidelity, Angelo probably thought he had every right to object to her friendship with Toby.

'But I don't like it,' Angelo countered flatly.

Absorbing the smouldering aspect of Angelo's intent gaze, Gwenna was surprised to feel an unexpected twinge of amusement. She dipped her head to hide it. He was so possessive, so incredibly passionate. He was not at all the cold, callous and insensitive guy she had once believed. 'I can see your point,' she answered with determined tact.

The savage tension in Angelo's broad shoulders eased.

'I wish you would stay awake, *passione mia*, 'Angelo complained.

'Can't…hardly slept last night,' she mumbled, all the stresses of the past forty-eight hours finally taking their toll. Her eyelids felt as though weights were attached to them.

He eased her between cool sheets and she waited for him to join her. Instead she heard a door open and she peered sleepily across the room at him, noting that his sleek bronzed length was clad only in boxers. 'Where are you going?'

'My room is through here.' He was poised on the threshold of the room next door.

Her pale brow indented. 'But—'

The smooth brown breadth of his muscular shoulders shifted in a casual shrug. 'I always sleep alone. I'll see you in the morning.'

The door closed. *I always sleep alone.* She had spent a lifetime sleeping alone too and could not comprehend why she should now feel rejected by his withdrawal. Exhaustion soon kicked in, however, to blur her troubled thoughts and sink her into a deep slumber.

She woke with a start, unsure of her surroundings and of what might have wakened her. In a rush she remembered that she was in Angelo's house and she fumbled for the light switch by the bed. She was sitting up when she heard a disturbing sound from his room. A cry? Without further thought she slid out of bed and snatched up the shirt he had left in a careless heap. Hastily donning it, she opened the communicating door between their rooms.

In the dawn light filtering through the shutters she could see Angelo tossing and turning in the big bed. He was moaning something in his own language. The sheer terror in his voice grabbed her by the throat, shook her up and sent her flying straight to his side. She scrambled up on the mattress to get within reach of him and rested a soothing hand on his shoulder. His skin was as hot as fire.

'Angelo…wake up!' she whispered urgently, shaking him slightly.

Angelo wrenched himself up in a sudden movement that startled her. He was trembling, muttering in Italian. With a gruff exclamation, he raked rough fingers through his dishevelled black hair and he turned to study her with a frown that drew his sleek ebony brows together. 'What are you doing here?'

'You were having a bad dream—'

'I don't get them—'

'You cried out and woke me up!'

'I couldn't have,' Angelo growled, dark eyes defensive, the fierce tension in his big powerful frame communicating itself to her.

Gwenna loosed a rueful sigh. Evidently, macho men didn't have bad dreams. In the dim light he was a dazzling bronzed vision of raw masculine appeal. With his hair ruffled and blue-black stubble outlining the aggressive set of his jaw line he looked startlingly handsome, but it was the grim cast of his lustrous eyes that made Gwenna shimmy closer on her bottom and wrap her arms round him. 'I get nightmares sometimes…'

'Really?' Angelo said very drily, but she noticed he didn't push her away.

Gwenna rested her chin on his shoulder, absently drinking in the warm and already familiar scent of his skin. 'I wasn't there when it happened but I used to dream I saw my mother's car crash. Then when I was at boarding-school—'

Angelo tensed. 'When was that?'

'I was ten when Dad first set up home with Eva and her daughters. Unfortunately, Penelope and Wanda didn't take to me and, for the sake of peace, I was sent off to school. I hated it.'

'Why…were you bullied?'

'For waking the other girls up with my nightmares and being a terrible cry-baby.' Gwenna winced in remembered shame over her past weakness. 'I was horribly homesick—'

Angelo reached behind him with a long arm and tipped her round and deftly forward into his lap. 'I was too, but I didn't have a home to go to any more.'

'You boarded too?'

'My mother was dead and her generous employer paid for my education at an exclusive school. I didn't fit in. Sardinian mothers spoil their sons. I spoke lousy English, and I was a science geek and very small—'

Gwenna squinted up at his shadowy profile. *'Small?'* she interrupted in disbelief.

Angelo nodded. 'Tiny…I didn't shoot up until I was well into my teens.'

'Were you bullied too?'

'Of course not.'

But Gwenna caught a certain intonation in his dark-timbred drawl and sighed. 'Yes, you *were*. I can tell.'

'How? With your crystal ball, *bella mia*?' Long, taunting fingers explored beneath the shirt she wore and she shivered, her breath catching in her throat.

'Stop trying to distract me…' she muttered breathlessly.

Angelo swung her down onto the bed beside him and shifted over her in one lithe motion, angling his hips into the soft cradle between her thighs to acquaint her with his thrusting hardness. Scorching eyes scorned her reproachful scrutiny. 'Is that what I'm doing?'

'But I want to know…I *really* want to know what happened to you to make you sound so scared!' she protested.

His fabulous bone structure clenched hard and he was pale. 'I was burned with cigarettes, kicked where it most hurts and beaten up.'

'Oh my word…' She was overcome by horror and consternation, and her eyes glistened, awash with moisture. 'Angelo…that's awful. And you still dream about it?'

'*Sì…*' Even as he wondered why the hell he had told her, Angelo was surveying her reaction in fascination.

Gwenna struggled to fight off the tears of sympathy without much success. She gulped, swallowed, sniffed and finally linked her arms tightly round him and hugged him hard. She was thinking of that bewildered and bright little boy, suddenly deprived of a loving mother and plunged into an alien environment.

'It made me tough…I was too soft, *bellezza mia*. It was good for me—'

'Don't talk rubbish!' Gwenna gasped, sucking in a steadying breath of oxygen. 'I mean, I was just teased and scolded. But you were brutalized—'

'Do you think I deserve a sympathy shag?' Angelo enquired in silken interruption.

Her clogged lashes lifted on troubled blue eyes. 'Sometimes you can be really offensive.'

Almost imperceptible colour scored his superb cheekbones.

'And the answer is no…not because I'm annoyed with you but because—and I find this very embarrassing—I think I would find it rather uncomfortable right now.' Grinding to a mortified halt as she referred to the fact that she was rather sore, she bit her lip and turned her face away.

Angelo hadn't thought of that possibility and guilt came out of nowhere and attacked him full force. It was less then forty-eight hours since she had been a virgin and he had been pretty demanding as well as passionate. Either he had a cold shower or he introduced her to a more creative way of satisfying his high sex drive.

'I can be selfish,' he remarked and waited confidently for her to argue that description.

But it did not even occur to Gwenna to contradict him for a statement she considered accurate. 'Maybe we could… later.'

'Later I'll be in New York, *cara mia*,' Angelo groaned in frustration, releasing her reluctantly from his weight but tugging her into his arms, fully intent on attacking her learning curve.

Gwenna squinted at the face of the clock by the bed and gasped. 'My goodness, is that the time?'

'It's only half past six,' Angelo told her gently.

'In less than an hour it'll be feeding time at the pet hotel and I don't want to be late,' she lamented, pulling free and rolling over to vacate his bed at a frantic pace. 'The staff don't mind me going to give Piglet breakfast because he wouldn't eat otherwise. But they do like me to fit in with their routine and they don't like visitors between eight and nine in the morning.'

Barely able to credit that harried explanation, Angelo sat up. 'Give me a moment,' he urged tautly. 'Are you telling me that you're running over there every single morning to feed that animal?'

'Evenings too…he has a very tiny tummy,' Gwenna told him defensively. 'You should see him on the webcam in his kennel…he's so depressed, it would break your heart. He won't even look at the TV or play ball any more.'

Her departure from his room was hasty. Angelo cursed vehemently while he took a cold shower and strode out of the wet room determined to get a look at Piglet malingering on the webcam. And there he was, the clever little tyke, curled up on his gilded four-poster bed with his head sunk between paws, little round eyes dull and his ridiculous bat ears drooping. In no need of canine acting lessons, he was the very picture of full-blown doggy misery.

But Gwenna was devoted to her pet. Totally devoted and obsessed, Angelo reflected dourly. And why not? How much love and attention had she got from her sleazy father and a mother who had probably only had her in an effort to destroy her lover's marriage? He lifted the phone. When Gwenna got out of his bed at dawn to trek across the city simply to feed the dog, it was time to release Piglet from captivity.

CHAPTER SEVEN

ANGELO surveyed the huge crowded room with concealed dissatisfaction. He wondered why it was that when fate gave him what he believed he had always wanted he should find it so irritating. Clingy women who remained welded to him like superglue in company had always exasperated him.

In the course of a month, he had learned that Gwenna did not cling, shadow him round the room or continually seek ways to attract his attention. In fact, he sometimes felt like handcuffing her to his wrist or tagging her with a satellite-navigation system he could use to locate her when he wanted her back by his side. When she got talking to his guests, she lost track of time. She was wildly popular with the garden enthusiasts and had to be regularly rescued from those who took advantage of her horticultural knowledge to request free advice and even personal visits.

'Where is she?' Angelo was finally forced to ask Franco.

A few minutes later, his chief of security at his heels, he strode out to the rear terrace of his impressive London abode and looked down into the garden below. Her iridescent blue evening gown trailing across the damp grass in her wake, Gwenna was showing off a flowering wall plant to a man and a woman. The man was a notoriously lecherous Swiss banker. That he should even be close to Gwenna set Angelo's teeth on edge.

Franco cleared his throat. 'You know, boss…Miss Hamilton doesn't know she might be rattling your cage.'

'Is that a fact?' Angelo murmured without expression.

'She's a very friendly lady, who loves helping people,' the older man remarked into the awkward silence.

So, that dangerous virus of niceness was subverting the loyalties of all the staff who came into regular contact with her, Angelo acknowledged sardonically. She took what Angelo considered to be an inordinate interest in other people and made no distinction between his employees and his acquaintances. Even Franco, a tough nut with a jaundiced view of the female sex, was eager to speak up on her behalf. His chauffeur, cured of a persistent cough with the gift of some magical mixture derived from honey, regarded her with positive reverence. His hard-hitting senior PA had mentioned how very pleasant and courteous Gwenna was. His chef conjured up special dishes adorned with horticultural motifs because she had planted herbs in containers for him.

Unfortunately, Angelo felt pretty much excluded from that general niceness and that awareness nagged at him like a fine stiletto knife in his side. She did not take an inordinate interest in him or question his absences. There was a barrier beyond which she did not go. But she *did* set him on fire in bed and wasn't that what was most important? he asked himself impatiently. Sometimes he joined her at dawn after an all-night meeting. No woman had ever given him so much pleasure and he went to great lengths to make time to be with her. He also gave her a lot of attention. Naturally he wanted her to be content with her role in his life and he was a very generous lover. But she was not responding to his efforts to gratify her.

She wore the clothes and the jewellery he gave her with indifference, shedding them for jeans and T-shirts the first opportunity she got. Film premières and fashionable parties did not impress her. Celebrities, the very few that she actually recognised, roused an equal lack of enthusiasm. His houses were a roof over her head, but no more, and only the outside spaces were capable of engaging any real interest. Hadn't he reunited her with her precious pet? Did he complain when that tiny psychologically disturbed mutt lay in wait to attack him? Piglet was the canine version of a piranha fish.

But what bothered Angelo most of all was the sneaking suspicion that Gwenna was not happy. She didn't brandish that unhappiness, never mentioned it and didn't droop in public. Yet he was continually conscious of it. Was she pining for Toby James? The very suspicion filled Angelo with a murderous tide of hostility. Infuriated by that lack of mental discipline, he used his fierce strength of will to thrust both the name and thought from his mind.

And if she was unhappy, Angelo was aware that he would soon be breaking news that would make her even unhappier. Three weeks ago, he had had a call from the lawyers he had instructed to check over every aspect of the properties that Donald Hamilton had signed over. Question marks had speedily been raised by certain anomalies in the paperwork and further extended investigation had revealed that Hamilton was guilty of yet another crime. Angelo now had the proof of an unscrupulous fraud that would destroy Gwenna's faith in her father for ever.

Her face pink from the attention Johannes Saudan was paying her and the dagger looks of resentment emanating from his girlfriend, Gwenna answered the middle-aged banker's query as briefly as she could. When she saw Angelo on the terrace above, it was a relief to be able to say, 'I think Angelo wants me...'

'What man would not? You are stunning.' The older man's appraisal made her feel horribly like a piece of meat on a slab.

'Excuse me.' Suppressing a shudder of revulsion, she headed back indoors.

Angelo strode in from the terrace to greet her. His brilliant gaze rested on hers and an erotic twist of instant heat shimmied through her pelvis. She stiffened, hating the weakness in her legs, the heavy feel of her breasts and the dulled hollow ache of response in a place she didn't care to think about. He owned her body, she thought wretchedly. He looked at her, he touched her and she would be seduced by her own weakness and craving. Physically he reigned supreme over her for she had yet to find a way of resisting him.

'I always have to look for you...even in my own house, *bellezza mia*,' Angelo murmured silkily.

It was a reproof but she bent her head, lowered her long curling pale brown lashes and said nothing. After all, what could she have said? She operated a deliberate policy of being elusive and could hardly complain if it exasperated him. In the bedroom she was always where he expected to find her because to her mind that, according to their agreement, was where their relationship began and ended.

He had sex with her. He had sex an awful lot with her. She was honest enough to admit that she was equally keen to have sex with him. She supposed that, in the circumstances, this was fortunate, but her anguished pride and her shame at what he had made of her would not allow her to award him much notice outside the bedroom door. She had resolved not to make a fuss about the physical stuff and not to act like the virtuous virgin he had once called her. Regrettably that did not make it any easier to deal with an inner turmoil that was growing stronger by the day. In every way that mattered, that agreement offended her beliefs and destroyed her self-respect.

'I would like to see a little more of you when we entertain,' Angelo spelt out in the same even tone as he lifted her slender hand.

'Okay.' Gwenna reminded herself that he had said nothing when Piglet chewed up one of his shoes. Either time it had happened. For a man who didn't like indoor animals he was being remarkably tolerant.

His thumb smoothed over the soft skin of her inner wrist and lingered. The faint aroma of her perfume flared his nostrils. Her pulse was going crazy. A slight tremor ran through her and the increased rapidity of her breathing stirred her breasts.

Madly conscious of the warmth of his skin against hers and of the electric sparks of awareness in the atmosphere, Gwenna glanced up at him. The dark pupils of her blue eyes were dilated. Sensual tension sizzled through her, holding her still. She was on a high and although she tried she could not pull back from that intoxicating sense of energy and power while his smouldering tawny eyes burned over her with masculine appreciation.

Angelo bent his arrogant dark head to murmur thickly, 'How do you do this to me?'

Taunting heat pulsed at the heart of her. She felt so wicked she closed her eyes tight, fighting his electrifyingly sexual magnetism. 'I don't know what you're talking about—'

'*Di niente.* Let me show you.' Snapping both hands over her wrists, Angelo backed into the room behind him and drew her with him.

The instant she registered his intention, Gwenna went

rigid. She knew that hot, intent look on his lean, darkly handsome face. It filled her with an excitement she loathed. All too often Angelo had proved to her how weak she was by choosing unconventional times and places to slake his passion and always she surrendered, too caught up in excitement to resist. But, for a split second, she had an image of how she would look emerging from the room with tousled hair and smudged make-up and she recoiled in shame from that prospect.

'No…not now. Your guests will notice we're missing.'

'So what?' Angelo curved lean, determined hands to her hips to jerk her into more intimate contact with his hard thighs.

'They'll guess what we've been doing—'

Angelo vented a low-pitched laugh of amusement. 'Why should they?'

But Gwenna had often seen herself in the mirror after their encounters, the feverish pink of her cheeks and the languorous daze in her eyes that told an all-too-intimate story. 'They *will*.'

'But why should we care about such things, *bellezza mia*?' Undaunted, Angelo reached up to undo the halter ties at the nape of her slender neck.

'No!' Angry distress gripping her, Gwenna thrust his hands away from the ties. 'You don't care and why should you? All the men will think you're a real ace, but I'll just look like a slapper!'

Angelo dealt her an incredulous appraisal. 'What has come over you? Where is all this nonsense coming from?'

'It's not nonsense. We really don't need to advertise what this relationship is about,' Gwenna slung back at him bitterly. 'And I won't be humiliated in front of smarmy creeps like Johannes Saudan!'

'What did Saudan say to you?' Angelo demanded angrily. 'How have I humiliated you?'

'Relax, Saudan didn't say anything, but I could see what he was thinking and he's not the only one—'

Angelo spread his hands in a slashing movement. 'Will you calm down and talk sense?'

'You put me on parade for them all like a prize poodle. The diamonds round my neck are the equivalent of a collar—'

'Isn't it amazing how many women look with envy on that collar?'

'It's like being branded by your ownership and I don't care how much moneys it's worth!' Gwenna practically spat at him. 'You just don't get it, do you? You think that being your playmate is some kind of honour—'

'*Santo Cielo!* Move away from that door,' Angelo instructed with chilling ferocity. 'I need to talk to Saudan about what he said to you.'

'I told you that he didn't *say* anything—he didn't need to! He believes I can be bought and, when he looked at me, I could see that he was wondering how soon you'd put me back on the market again. Because to him I'm just a commodity and he was thinking that he could have me too—'

Angelo lifted her bodily out of his path. 'I'll bloody kill him!'

'What for?' she demanded wildly.

'*Dannazione!* He upset you,' Angelo grated.

Afraid of a scene, she stepped in front of the door to prevent his exit. 'Why should you care about that?' Without the slightest warning her voice had developed a wobble and tears were drenching her eyes.

Angelo loathed female tears like poison and never, ever let himself be swayed by tantrums. But when he saw those sparkling drops on Gwenna's lashes he felt as hugely relieved, as if she had provided him with a list of instructions on how he should respond. She was upset, crying. He could not possibly take offence at anything she had said. The raging frustration inside him immediately subsided. Suddenly everything seemed simple and his own function wonderfully clear-cut. He rested his hands on her shoulders and in a clever series of stealthy moves slowly and gently eased her shivering slender length into his arms.

A sob convulsed Gwenna's throat and she gulped it back hurriedly. 'I don't cry…I don't—'

'I don't hear you crying,' Angelo breathed, wondering if he was a pervert for just wanting to kick out all his guests and drag her up to bed and keep her there for at least twenty-four hours.

She rested her brow against a broad shoulder. She felt totally bewildered by her own behaviour. How had she ended up so close to him? The angry pain that had taken her over had gone and she recognised a disconcerting change in her attitude to him. Arguing with Angelo had once made her feel stronger and more in control but this time around it had made her feel as if she were being torn in two.

'I'm all right,' she muttered awkwardly just as her mobile phone rang. 'Excuse me…'

It was her stepsister, Penelope.

'We need to talk to you urgently,' Penelope declared in a sharp voice that made Gwenna's heart sink like a stone and her anxiety level rise even faster. 'It's a family matter and I can't discuss it on the phone. How quickly can you get down here?'

'I'll get on the first available train tomorrow.'

'I have to go home for a couple of days,' Gwenna told Angelo, anxiously wondering if the problem that her stepsister had refused to discuss related to the total breakdown of their respective parents' marriage. 'It's a family crisis.'

His lean, strong face austere, Angelo frowned. 'I'll come with you.'

Gwenna was painfully conscious of Angelo's attitude to her father, and could only think that Angelo's presence would increase the strain and embarrassment for all concerned. 'Thanks, but I don't think that's a good idea. This is private family stuff.'

Angelo thought that was doubtful. Most probably Donald Hamilton was in serious trouble again. When Angelo had exposed the older man's thefts from Furnridge Leather, he had known that it would only be a matter of time until further crimes were laid at Hamilton's door. Other people's suspicions and worries would almost inevitably lead to an investigation of Donald Hamilton's other financial dealings. He studied Gwenna's pale, troubled profile and marvelled that she could still be so vulnerable and naïve. He thought it was past time that she appreciated that her parent was a greedy, lying con man without a conscience.

'Do you think you could look after Piglet?' Gwenna asked uncomfortably. 'It's just my stepmother doesn't like dogs and I think he would be traumatised if he was put back into the pet hotel.'

Angelo felt oddly humbled by her trust in him as regards her pet, for there was no doubt that Piglet was her most precious possession. '*Non c'è problema*...no problem.'

He closed a strong, tanned hand over hers. A wave of unidentifiable emotion was washing about inside Gwenna. She wanted to lean on him but she wouldn't let herself and could not explain why such a strange prompting should assail her.

'When I take you home later we'll make it a night to remember, *bellezza mia*,' Angelo husked, turning her insides to a delicious jelly of shameless anticipation.

Early the following morning, she wakened and listened to Angelo moving about in the room next door. He never spent the whole night with her. He always slept alone. Yet he gave her the most unimaginable pleasure…

Angelo strode in. Fully dressed in a very snazzy designer business suit and looking devastatingly handsome, he came to a halt at the foot of the bed. Her torrent of warm honey-coloured hair was an exotic tangle that framed her heart-shaped face and accentuated her glorious blue eyes and luscious pink mouth.

'*Dio mio*…I'm not sure I can let you go, *cara mia*,' Angelo breathed and he was only half joking. 'You were amazing last night.'

Although she reddened, Gwenna shifted between the sheets like a sinuous cat being stroked by silk. His purring intonation and the hot glow of his hungry gaze made her feel empowered, but she was shocked when she heard herself say, 'You should've stayed…'

'I have a meeting in an hour,' he intoned huskily. 'It's very important.'

The sexual buzz in the air tingled through Gwenna like a shot of adrenalin. She studied his stunning dark features from below her lashes, crystalline blue eyes limpid.

It was the first time Gwenna had given him a come-on and Angelo felt dizzy with sheer lust and triumph. He called Franco and murmured in slightly ragged Italian, 'Inform the office that I've been unavoidably detained.'

He loosened the knot of his tie with an air of purpose and shed it along with his jacket. Not once did he remove his striking gaze from her perplexed face. He released the buttons on his shirt with taunting slowness.

Gwenna was paralysed by surprise and the dulled heavy sensation of warmth low in her belly. 'What are you doing? Your meeting…'

Angelo came down on the bed beside her and reached for her with confident hands. 'Make missing it worth my while,' he invited in erotic challenge, letting his tongue delve deep between her parted lips and ravish the sweetness from her soft mouth.

Around noon, he shook her awake. She blinked up at him like a rabbit caught in headlights, still so exhausted that her body literally felt weighted to the mattress. Angelo on the other hand looked re-energised. His black hair was still wet and spiky from the shower, his beautiful eyes brilliant as diamonds above his superb bronzed cheekbones. 'You've missed your train. A driver is standing by to take you to the heliport. You can fly down to see your family. Don't stay away too long.'

Gwenna never woke up quickly and she was as flustered by the wild passion that had exploded between them as by the prospect of being flown by helicopter to Somerset. 'Okay…'

Angelo carried her fingers to his handsome mouth and kissed them in a mocking gesture that made her tense up even more. Straightening, he surveyed her with wolfish satisfaction. 'Congratulations, *bellezza mia*.'

Gwenna gave him a bemused look. 'For what?'

'You finally feel like you belong to me.'

Gwenna went white.

'That's how I wanted it and how it has to be. There was never any way that I was going to settle for less,' Angelo imparted silkily. 'What price true love now? You're more mine than you could ever be his.'

Angelo strolled out the door whistling quietly. Gwenna stared into space, a sick sense of humiliation coruscating through her. In the grip of a frantic surge of tempestuous emotion, she leapt out of bed, snatched up her dressing gown and hurtled to the door to bawl. 'Angelo?'

Angelo came to a lazily graceful halt on the landing and swung round to regard her from below dense black lashes in mocking enquiry. 'Yes…?'

'Who do you think I'm thinking about whenever I'm with you?' she hurled and even as she said it she cringed for herself. Such spite and such lying were unfamiliar to her, but every time Angelo hurt her she found herself reacting in unpredictable ways.

Angelo stared steadily back at her, eyes black as pitch, lean, strong face expressionless. She saw his loss of colour and knew her nasty retaliation had hit home. Yet she was more ashamed and troubled than pleased by her success. She felt the sudden dangerous drop in temperature and she shivered, afraid and full of regret.

Reeling back into the bedroom, she leant back against the door to close it and covered her clammy face with trembling hands. What was happening to her? What had he done to her?

When had thoughts of Toby even entered her head in Angelo's presence? Not once. That belated realisation shocked and frightened her…

CHAPTER EIGHT

'YOU travel in luxury: a private helicopter for your sole use and a limo and driver to deliver you right to our door?' Donald Hamilton awarded Gwenna an admiring smile across the depth of his spacious book-lined study. 'I'm impressed. Obviously, Angelo Riccardi thinks very highly of you.'

'I don't know about that. I just missed my train.' Gwenna was already wondering if Penelope had exaggerated the family crisis because her father did not seem unduly concerned. Indeed he seemed quite relaxed. 'Penelope made the situation here sound grave and she was very mysterious. I've been really worried.'

'Then you'll be relieved to learn that my current problem is only what you might call a footnote to that other business at Furnridge.' The older man grimaced. 'There I was in a hell of a bind and I did what most people in a financial crisis do— I borrowed just a little from Peter to pay Paul.'

Gwenna tensed again. 'Meaning…er, sorry, I don't quite understand.'

'I'm afraid that certain irregularities in the garden committee's accounts have been uncovered. Of course, given time I could make all good.' Donald shrugged. 'Unfortunately the stuffy old worrywarts on the committee are demanding instant repayment.'

'You took money from the Massey Garden Fund…*as well*?' Gwenna was appalled when she finally grasped the gravity of what she was being told. 'What on earth were you thinking of?'

'I don't care for your tone, Gwenna,' her father censured with a lofty look of reproof.

'I just can't believe that after all that fund-raising and all those speeches you actually helped yourself to the donations of the people who trusted you,' she whispered painfully, shame weighing her down like a giant piece of concrete. 'Why didn't you mention this last month?'

'Obviously because I hoped to be in a position to replace the money. But that's since proved impossible. I'm unemployed, and Eva and I can barely afford to live in this house. Two members of the garden committee called yesterday. They're threatening to call in the police.'

Her brow felt as though a tension band was tightening round it. 'How much money are we talking about?'

Donald winced and mentioned a sum that shook her rigid.

'Oh, my word…what are we going to do?' she exclaimed.

'Well, possibly you could sell a diamond necklace or something to save our skins,' a female voice interposed with very female venom.

Gwenna looked up in dismay to see her stepsisters and her stepmother coming into the room.

'Or, you could simply *ask* your fabulously rich lover to bail your father out,' Penelope continued in the same sarcastic tone.

'I can't do that,' Gwenna whispered sickly, not knowing how to explain that she did not consider herself the owner of any of the diamond jewellery that Angelo had insisted she wear.

'Sadly, you're the only person who can help me now,' her father told her heavily. 'We have no money and no hope of getting a loan.'

And with that final comment, Donald Hamilton left the room.

'I can't do anything,' Gwenna said again. 'I don't have any money either.'

Eva spoke up for the first time. 'If you don't find the means to sort this out discreetly, I assure you that I will divorce your father and then he won't even have anywhere to live. I've had enough. I won't tolerate any more.'

Gwenna sighed heavily. 'I can understand how you feel—'

'I don't think you do. While our lives have been crashing and burning as we struggled to pay our bills, you've been swanning down red carpets to film premières!' Penelope condemned furiously. 'I see your picture in all the top magazines and your name in the gossip columns. You're shacked up with a Category-A billionaire!'

'It would have been crude to present Angelo with a shopping list of demands in your very first week,' Wanda opined, 'but it's time you stopped being selfish and shared your amazing good fortune with your family.'

'That's enough, girls,' their mother, Eva, murmured. 'I'm quite sure that Gwenna has got the message.'

In shock from that combined verbal attack, Gwenna was hit even harder by the pure injustice of the allegations of selfishness.

'I don't believe that finding the money will be a problem for you,' Penelope remarked sweetly. 'After all, you're wearing a fortune on your back. That handbag alone must be worth fifteen hundred pounds!'

Gwenna stared down at her bag in horror. Did bags come that expensive? She had not a clue what any of her clothing or accessories had cost, for the simple reason that she had not shopped for them personally and they had not been delivered with price tags attached. She now deeply regretted raiding her designer wardrobe in an effort to boost her confidence in advance of an encounter with her sharp-tongued stepsisters.

'I don't have any money of my own and I can't ask Angelo for it,' she argued tautly, her mind in turmoil.

Her stepmother wrinkled her nose. From what I've seen, Angelo Riccardi needs very little encouragement to spoil you rotten.'

Angry, frustrated tears blinding her, Gwenna leapt to her feet. 'Stop talking like I'm with Angelo out of choice! Or like it was some big treat for me! I was in love with someone else, for goodness' sake. Angelo offered me a deal—if I slept with him, he would drop the charges against Dad!'

No sooner had the words left Gwenna's lips than she regretted an admission that she would never have made had she not been so upset and desperate to defend herself. Silence had fallen. All three women were now viewing her with dropped jaws of disbelief and she was totally mortified.

'I had no idea,' Eva retorted frigidly. 'It sounds absolutely immoral and I hope you're not blaming us for your decision. Do we need the sordid details?'

'Angelo Riccardi had to *blackmail* you into bed with him?' Wanda gasped wide-eyed. 'I'd have knocked him flat in the rush. What's the matter with you?'

'That is so, *so* sexy.' Penelope could not conceal her envy. 'You are really sad, Gwenna. No normal woman would be moaning about it!'

Dumbfounded by those reactions, Gwenna walked out of the room. She was taken aback to see Toby waiting in the hall. Just as quickly she appreciated that Toby, as a member of the garden committee, would already have been informed that her father had taken money from the restoration fund.

'I only found out about this yesterday. I volunteered to break the news to you and I couldn't do it on the phone. I meant to make it here before you but my flight was delayed,' Toby confided apologetically.

'Gwenna…' Donald Hamilton spoke from the far end of the hall in an admonishing tone.

'Get me out of here,' Gwenna begged her oldest friend in a frantic whisper, before turning back to address her father. 'I don't know what to say to you right now. I need to think things over. Please don't expect me to pull off a miracle. I'll be in touch.'

Ignoring the older man's protests, Toby ushered her quickly out to his car. 'Look, I'm booked in at the Four Crowns inn for the night. Why don't we go there to talk?'

Her mobile phone was buzzing. It was Angelo calling. *He was still talking to her, then.* But her surge of guilty relief was short-lived when she contemplated telling Angelo about her parent's latest act of embezzlement. Mentally shrinking from that ghastly challenge, she switched off her phone. When they arrived at the Four Crowns, Toby confessed that he hadn't eaten for hours and added that, as far as he knew, starving had never solved a crisis. Neither of them mentioned the theft over a late dinner. Afterwards they went up to his comfortable room with its ancient oak beams to talk over a bottle of wine.

'I'll be blunt. The committee is champing at the bit to call in the police but I persuaded them to hold off for another day or so. They don't want the scandal of this going public in case it inhibits further donations to the fund,' Toby explained. '*Is* Angelo likely to bail your dad out?'

Gwenna swallowed hard. 'I doubt it—Angelo won't be sympathetic.'

'But Angelo struck me as keen on you.'

Gwenna reddened because she didn't feel that she could point out that her sole value in Angelo's terms was of a highly physical nature. And that after the lie she had flung at Angelo earlier, even that low measure of her worth had probably hit rock-bottom.

'I won't say what I'd like to say about your father.'

'I appreciate that…' Gwenna flinched nervously as a knock sounded on the door.

Toby opened the door. Gwenna saw Angelo and her heart reacted as if it were jumping right out of her chest. She jumped to her feet, Dclft-blue eyes locking in sudden fear to the icy black outrage flaming in Angelo's glittering gaze. As she moved forward Angelo hit Toby, who went flying backwards to fall against the side of the bed.

'Are you insane?' Gwenna shrieked.

'You were lying on his bed!' Angelo gritted. 'Stay out of this. This is between me and him—'

'I'm not a coward, but I've just never seen the point of all that macho shouting and thumping stuff,' Toby groaned, hugging his ribs and struggling to catch his breath.

Angelo studied him in incredulous disgust. 'He won't even fight for you!'

'Why would he fight for me? He's gay,' Gwenna said woodenly, crouching down beside Toby to ask him if he was all right.

'Gay?' Angelo thundered in disbelief.

'Gay,' Toby confirmed, squinting at Gwenna in surprise and then back at Angelo. 'Didn't she mention it?'

'It was none of Angelo's business,' Gwenna declared, refusing to look at either man.

Angelo strode forward and immediately extended a hand down to Toby to help the younger man up. 'I'm sorry. I owe you a sincere apology.' He sent Gwenna a shimmering glance of challenge. 'Why didn't you tell me? How wasn't it my business?'

Her cheeks flushed a discomfited pink, Gwenna folded her lips on a stinging retort. A slanging match in front of Toby in which Angelo was certain to give as good as he got would only embarrass her more. She already felt foolish, angry and guilty that Toby had got hurt. She did not want to recall that, when she first realised that Angelo had followed her down to Somerset, she had been pleased.

'Are you coming back to my hotel with me?' Angelo drawled softly.

Gwenna jerked her chin in grudging affirmation. 'How could you do that?' she snapped the minute she was alone with Angelo.

'You're responsible for that stupid farce,' Angelo drawled with cutting cool, thrusting open the inn door for her to precede him into the car park.

'And how do you make that out?' Gwenna demanded.

'You didn't answer your mobile phone. You walked out of your father's house with the man you told me you loved. You then dined alone with him and went upstairs to his hotel room. What was I supposed to think?'

'That not everyone is as oversexed as you are!'

Gay! The guy was gay! Why hadn't she said? Angelo's aggressive jaw line squared. She was all sweetness and light with everyone else, but she had gone out of her way to put him through the equivalent of a meat mincer. Subtle torture of the most female kind. Naturally he had found it offensive that her main source of interest should be another man, when it was *his* bed she was sharing! When she had thrown that fact in his teeth earlier that day, Angelo had been dismayed by the discovery that he was struggling to restrain his temper even with his staff.

'I still don't understand how you knew where I was today.'

Angelo dealt her a sardonic look. 'I always know where you are. Whenever you go out, someone on Franco's team watches over you. I'm in the public eye. I have enemies. Even if the only threat is from the paparazzi, you need protection.'

Gwenna could hardly contain her annoyance. 'It's like being under police surveillance…why didn't you tell me?'

'Your safety is my concern. So, tell me the tale of Toby,' Angelo invited, determined to satisfy his curiosity. 'How did you manage to fall for someone who's gay?'

Gwenna worried at her lower lip with her teeth before she finally answered. 'It was a secret and I wasn't in on it when I first knew him. By the time I found out, it was too late.'

'How too late? Finding out *that* should have been a wake-up call,' Angelo said very drily.

'It's not that simple—'

'In the same scenario I would find it very simple.'

Gwenna tilted her chin. 'When did you last fall for anyone?'

Angelo felt as if he had been dumped in conversational quicksand. He didn't do love, didn't believe in it, didn't go into the building, never mind the living room. Love was a four-letter word that had never crossed his lips since childhood and not something he was prepared to talk about. His icy reserve was well known. People didn't ask him personal questions. They didn't have the nerve. They didn't want to irritate him.

'How come you can ask me but I can't ask you?' she prompted in the simmering silence.

'*Dio mio*…I don't fall. Okay?'

Gwenna fixed stunned china-blue eyes on him. 'You mean…*ever*?'

'So what?' Angelo was infuriated by her compassionate look that implied he must be some kind of emotional cripple.

Gwenna wished she hadn't asked. She felt terribly sad for him and hastened to breach the awkward silence. 'My grandmother used to say that it takes all sorts to make a world,' she continued brightly. 'I suppose that if I'd ever met anyone else worth caring about, I would've got over Toby. There again, he would be a hard act to follow. He's very creative—he designs parks and gardens. We have a lot in common—'

'Soil...plants...' Angelo slotted in with lethal derision. 'The wow factor.'

Her heart-shaped face tightened. 'Toby's really special—kind and caring.'

Worth caring about. Although he wasn't looking for love, Angelo felt affronted. Toby was kind, caring and creative. It was not a level playing field. Possibly Toby filled in for the saints in his spare time. Angelo decided that pursuing the topic was beneath his dignity.

It was almost midnight when they arrived at the Peveril House hotel. A private lift whisked them up to an opulent suite that comprised several rooms. Gwenna had taken one step through the door when Piglet hurled himself at her in rapturous welcome.

'My word, you brought him with you!' Gwenna pounced happily on her pet. 'Thank you.'

Angelo wondered how he was supposed to have left behind a dog that went on hunger strike without her. Piglet had to be the most successful attention-seeker in canine history.

The next morning, Gwenna woke up at nine. In spite of everything she had slept like a log and Angelo had left her undisturbed. Totally undisturbed. Maybe he had realised how exhausted she had been. She was surprised that he hadn't asked about the nature of her family crisis the night before. But then why should he be interested? But if he wasn't interested, why had he followed her down to Somerset?

She could no longer avoid the disagreeable decision she had to make. Did she or did she not ask Angelo to help her father? Certainly, she didn't want to make that approach. In fact she cringed at the very thought of it. But although Eva and her daughters had been unpleasant and her father had treated the matter far too lightly, Gwenna still felt that she should do what she could to try and help. The money had been taken from the garden fund around the same time as the money from Furnridge. In many ways it could be seen as another strand of the same offence, she told herself bracingly.

When she appeared for breakfast, Angelo acknowledged her with an inclination of his handsome dark head. He was poised by a desk across the room and talking in rapid Italian, and it was clear to her that he was fully engaged in business. She watched him covertly while she chased some cereal round a bowl, her appetite steadily dwindling at the prospect of the dialogue that lay ahead.

Angelo tossed the phone aside and strolled fluidly towards her. In a well-cut suit the colour of rich caramel, a silk shirt and a narrow trendy tie, he was drop-dead beautiful, she acknowledged helplessly.

'Sleep well?' he enquired casually.

'Yes…thanks.'

'I didn't.' Lean, powerful face intent, Angelo lounged back against the table edge. He watched her with a smouldering intensity that spoke louder than any words. Slow, painful colour inched up her pale, slender throat and into her cheeks and she didn't ask him why he hadn't slept well because she knew. 'Come here,' he breathed softly.

And she lifted out of her chair before she even appreciated that she was going to move. With a husky sound of amusement, Angelo curved an assured hand to her hip and looked her up and down with bold visual appreciation. 'I picked out that dress for you in New York.'

Gwenna was surprised. 'I didn't know you picked anything.'

Angelo was wholly engaged in admiring the enchanting picture she made. The dress was a perfect fit for her luscious curves and the exact same shade of blue as the one she had worn the day they met. 'Only a couple of items that caught my eye. I've decided that we need a break, *bellezza mia*,' he imparted. 'We're flying to Sardinia at the end of the week.'

'Are you serious?' Gwenna exclaimed.

'I have a house there…a huge garden,' Angelo tossed in for good measure. 'You'll love it and so will I. Like your plants, I need copious amounts of sunlight and attention to thrive.'

Gwenna studied him uncertainly. 'Don't you want to know why I needed to see my family yesterday?'

Angelo released his breath in a slow, expressive hiss. 'I have a fair idea.'

Her smooth brow furrowed. 'How? I mean…you didn't say anything,' she faltered.

'How? I have senior staff at Furnridge and the rumours about the depredations on the local garden fund hit the grapevine there a few days ago,' Angelo confided with precision. 'I then made further enquiries, which is why I'm here.'

'It's not just a rumour.'

Level dark eyes gazed steadily down at her. 'I didn't think it would be.'

Gwenna moistened her dry lips. 'My father took the money and used it to try and conceal the sums he had taken from Furnridge.'

Angelo lifted his hand to skate a warning forefinger gently across her full lower lip. 'Let's not have this conversation. I don't like the direction I suspect it might be taking.'

Her lashes fluttered up on her bemused gaze. 'How am I supposed to answer that?'

'Hopefully with a change of subject. Your life has moved on.'

'You don't just move on from family.'

His lean face was sombre. 'You could be surprised.'

'You *knew* about this and you didn't even mention it last night?' Gwenna shook her head in genuine confusion. 'No wonder you didn't ask me what was wrong! How do you keep things in separate compartments like that?'

'I'm a practical guy,' Angelo quipped.

'But just to ignore the whole issue like that…'

Angelo lifted and dropped a broad shoulder in silence.

Gwenna could feel the chill in the air. She also noticed that he was no longer touching her. 'Angelo…'

'Don't go there, *bellezza mia*,' Angelo cautioned.

Gwenna spun away from him and turned round again in a troubled half-circle. 'You can't know what I'm about to say before I've even said it!'

'Can't I?' Angelo countered bleakly.

'You're making this very hard for me. Do you think I find it easy to ask you for money?' she prompted unevenly and then groaned out loud. 'And now I'm making a mess of it.'

'Not at all. You've packaged yourself very prettily for the challenge. No jeans and T-shirt in sight,' Angelo derided softly.

Gwenna scrutinised him in sincere shock. 'You really think that that's why I'm dressed like this? I'm packaging myself? I'm not like that—'

'I thought you weren't like that too. Sadly, you seem set on course to prove me wrong.'

Pale and taut, Gwenna stilled, her eyes full of strain. 'Stop being clever and trying to scare me into silence. Don't you understand that I can't *not* ask?'

'No, I don't. Do you honestly believe that your father is a deserving cause? A truly penitent sinner worthy of a helping hand?'

His cold contempt lashed stinging colour into her cheeks. 'He's my father and I love him. Just at present, I'm ashamed of him too,' she confided with a catch in her low-pitched voice. 'He's weak and he's broken the law and he's betrayed the trust of others, but he's still my closest living relative—and I can't forget how he stood by me when I was a child.'

Angelo vented a harsh laugh. 'And what if he didn't stand by you in quite the way you imagine?'

Gwenna gazed back at him in bewilderment. 'What do you mean?'

Angelo veiled his granite hard gaze. She would have to deal with the truth some time. But now when she was already upset would be very poor timing. He would tell her in Sardinia and that would cut her loose. Like most con men, Hamilton was a seasoned liar and his life had more sordid secrets than a soap opera. Once she had been made to face the reality, she would soon rethink her sentimental take on family ties. And although he thought it regrettable that she would lose that trusting naivety in the process, he was determined to do it.

Gwenna laced her fingers through each other and threw back her slight shoulders as she steeled herself. 'I desperately want my father to have the chance to turn his life around—'

Angelo threw up his hands in a gesture of total derision and walked over to the window to turn his back on her. 'Oh…please,' he said acidly.

'He'll never do it if nobody believes in him. He'll go to prison if the garden committee has to press charges and wha choice do they have? Some very influential people donated money to the fund. Please consider replacing the money,' she whispered shakily. 'Even as a loan.'

'*Dio mio*… A loan with what security?' Angelo swung back and rested sardonic dark-as-night eyes on her. 'You almost had me convinced that you were different and I liked that idea. A lady with principles. Until now you had the unique distinction of being the only woman who has never asked me for money… Or jewels to the value of.'

The blood drained from below her fine creamy skin. She wanted to sink through the floor in shame and could not sustain his challenging gaze. The line that divided right from wrong was no longer as well defined as she had once believed it to be. Even while she felt bound in duty to try and protect her father, she was appalled by what she was doing.

'You also told me that you couldn't be bought,' Angelo reminded her darkly. 'But you just named your price.'

Hot, prickly tears hit the backs of her eyes. 'Angelo…I really didn't want to do this—'

'Yet you did. If I wanted to play games, I could ask you what's in it for me. But it would be cruel to put you on the spot when I have no intention of giving you a positive response. Do I care what happens to your father? No. Do I wish to please you to that extent? I'm afraid not,' Angelo completed with chilling cool.

That final assertion hurt as much as an unexpected slap in the face. It was one thing to tell herself that her sole value to Angelo Riccardi was sexual, quite another to be confronted with his unapologetic confirmation of the fact. Indeed he was so cold, so unemotionally distant, that he frightened her. It was as though the last month hadn't happened and he had reassumed the guise of a callous stranger.

Gwenna straightened her taut shoulders. 'I'm sorry I made the mistake of believing that you might have some compassion.'

'I reserve compassion for worthy causes and your father will never feature in that category.'

'Yet you can squander a fortune on stupid clothes for me! Hang diamonds worth…whatever round my neck!' she protested in a feverish rush of incomprehension. 'Even the way you sneer at me for caring about what happens to my father—'

'I don't sneer—'

'Your voice does it for you!'

'Your father is trying to use you again. Where's your common sense? Can't you tell? Does a decent man let his daughter pay for his freedom with her body?' Angelo raked at her with derision.

Gwenna gulped. 'That's not fair. Dad thinks we're really involved—'

'We are *really* involved—'

'You know what I mean. He thinks we *care* about each other,' she shot back wretchedly. 'And since you said it first—does a decent man ask a woman to pay for her father's freedom with her body?'

Outrage flashed in Angelo's punitive appraisal. '*Per meraviglia.* Don't pair me with your father in the same sentence. If people could still be bought and sold like goods, he'd be the first to sell you to me at a profit!'

'That's a filthy lie! My father loves me—'

'He's a con man and a swindler,' Angelo sliced in with cutting hauteur. 'I've an even better question for you to ask yourself. What sort of man steals his eight-year-old daughter's inheritance from her?'

Her feathery brows lifting in a frown of incomprehension,

Gwenna stared back steadily at him. 'What are you saying? I'm sorry…what's that supposed to mean? What inheritance?'

Lean, darkly handsome features taut, Angelo swore under his breath for he had not intended to reveal that information. 'Donald Hamilton forged his own version of your mother's will.'

It took so much effort to concentrate that Gwenna felt dizzy. 'Forged? I beg your pardon?'

'There's a lot of solid evidence. Handwriting experts have been consulted. The will is not even a clever fake. One witness and the solicitor involved have since died,' Angelo explained. 'The second witness, however, has been tracked down abroad and he's prepared to swear that the will is not the document he originally signed in your mother's presence. Your father forged another will and named himself as the main beneficiary. He wanted the Massey Manor estate and he took advantage of your mother's death to steal it from you.'

Gwenna was shaking her head back and forth like a metronome. 'This is nonsense, totally ridiculous nonsense—'

'And when your father rushed to offer you a home and adopt you, everybody was surprised but impressed. Nor did anyone ask why a woman who had been known to have hated him would have left him everything she possessed.'

'Angelo…this is wicked, what you're trying to insinuate, what you're saying,' Gwenna told him jerkily, words and phrases getting jumbled as she attempted unsuccessfully to master her shock.

'It's the truth.'

'No…no, it can't be.' Gwenna grabbed up her bag from the seat where she had left it the night before and hauled out her phone.

'Who are you calling?'

'Toby.'

Angelo snatched the phone off her. 'What do you need with him?'

'Give me my phone!' Gwenna screeched at him.

'Think before you spill the beans…can you trust Toby James with such highly sensitive information?' Angelo set her phone down on the table between them as though it were a very dangerous weapon. 'He's on that garden committee, isn't he?'

Gwenna snatched up her phone but she did not make the call. She wanted to hit Angelo for making her think twice about contacting her best friend for support. Her throat was thick with emotion. 'Dad did not forge my mother's will and this entire issue is nothing to do with you.'

'He signed over the property against his debt to Furnridge. If he didn't legally own the estate, he committed another act of fraud. Perhaps you would prefer the police to investigate the matter.'

A chill settled over Gwenna then. She felt as if she were trapped in a nightmare from which there was no escape. Angelo settled a hand to her spine. She pulled away in a violent movement of rejection.

'You had to be told some time, *bellezza mia.*'

Gwenna shot him a defiant glance. 'I intend to discuss your insane allegations with my father.'

'You should see the evidence first.' Angelo removed a file from the drawer of the desk and walked back to hand it to her.

'Go away,' she urged unevenly.

Angelo went out to the hall where Piglet had been corralled in disgrace. The little dog's morning walk had concluded with the noisy harassment of a driver climbing out of his car. Angelo had been quite heartened when he'd heard about that unprovoked attack. It was good to know that he wasn't the only man that Piglet hated. Purposefully leaving the door back into the drawing room ajar, Angelo watched Piglet take the bait and pelt past him to join Gwenna with a triumphant burst of barking.

Clutching her pet below one arm, Gwenna sat down at the desk and opened the file. There were legal letters, samples of her mother's signature, expert opinions. But when she came on the deposition from the man who had witnessed her mother's will, her tummy turned queasy. The witness was prepared to swear in court that Isabel Massey had left her estate to her child.

When Angelo reappeared half an hour later, Gwenna was proud that she had hung onto her composure. She stood up. 'I want to see my father.'

'He'll give you a pack of excuses. My staff tell me that that's how he operates,' Angelo advanced.

'I can handle it.' Her blue eyes were bright as stars with defiance as she looked steadily back at him.

'I'm sorry but I can't agree.'

'What the hell has it got to do with you?' she practically screamed at him, the sudden uncontrollable flare of her temper taking her by storm and shocking her.

Angelo remained tactfully silent.

'You think I'm going to lose it. Well, I'm not going to. I only lose it with you!' she muttered defensively.

Gwenna sat in the limo like a stone statue, but below the surface she was seething with a mess of disturbed emotions. The vehicle pulled up outside her father's home.

'You don't have to confront him. Why don't you let me deal with this?' Angelo asked levelly.

'He's *my* father.' Clutching the file, Gwenna climbed out. 'And don't you dare come in!'

CHAPTER NINE

DONALD HAMILTON leafed frantically through the file Gwenna had presented him with. Finally he thrust it down on the table. His complexion had taken on an unhealthy grey hue, his shock palpable. 'Did Angelo Riccardi put all that stuff together for you?'

'Yes,' Gwenna breathed. 'Please. I need to hear the truth.'

'It looks a lot worse than it is,' Donald declared defensively. 'Let me explain how it happened—'

'Don't talk as though it was something that you had no control over,' Gwenna broke in tautly. 'You forged my mother's will so that I was left penniless. That's what it comes down to!'

'You're making too much of this,' the older man argued vehemently. 'It all started out quite innocently. When you were a baby, I tried to persuade your mother, Isabel, into a business partnership. I hoped that together we could build houses on the Massey estate.'

'Build?' Gwenna parroted. 'But it's against the law to develop a site that's been listed as being of historical significance.'

'It was over twenty years ago and the estate wasn't listed then,' he reminded her doggedly. 'I wanted to make some money for us all. Isabel was as poor as a church mouse, but she went crazy when I suggested the property deal. Playing lady of the manor, even if the big house was in ruins, was very important to your mother.'

'By the time you were born, my relationship with Isabel was only a friendship,' Donald Hamilton contended.

That was not how Gwenna remembered it. The affair had waxed and waned according to her father's mood. Her mother's bitterness had escalated when she had finally begun to appreciate that the man she had loved for so long had never cared for her the way she cared for him.

'My first marriage was a disaster and I wanted a divorce. Developing the Massey estate seemed like my only escape route,' the older man continued with determination. 'I needed to make a lot of money. I had a wife to keep, I had you and your mother to support and, by then, I'd also met another woman.'

Gwenna could not say that she was surprised by that admission. 'Didn't that happen to you rather too often? Off with the old, on with the new?'

Her father grimaced. 'I don't expect you to understand but Fiorella was different. She was an Italian, very glamorous. I hoped to marry her but that affair blew up in my face—'

Gwenna frowned. 'I don't see what all this has got to do with my mother's will.'

'I'm trying to explain why I did what I did.'

Gwenna stared at the damning file, which lay on the coffee table. Beneath the table, Piglet sighed in his sleep. She was beginning to wonder why she had even bothered coming to see her father. She felt empty. Nothing he could say was going to make her feel better about the fact that he had stolen her birthright and held onto it for so many years at her expense. He had allowed her to believe that her adoption had led to his divorce. Yet he had just admitted that he had wanted out of that marriage.

Things she had closed her eyes to, comparisons that it hurt to make, were now crowding in on her. Her stepsisters had grown up in a lovely big house with their mother and her father, while Gwenna had been exiled to a down-market boarding-school that she'd hated. During the holidays, her presence in her father's marital home had been barely tolerated by her stepfamily. From the age of eighteen, she had lived in a cramped and shabby little flat that was basically just the roof space above a glorified shed of a shop and she had run the nursery for a meagre wage. Yet a mere word of approbation from her father had been sufficient to keep her walking on air for days afterwards.

'Gwenna…' Donald Hamilton spoke with unusual urgency. 'You have to listen to me.'

'If you want me to listen, tell me something relevant. The story of your romance with some glamorous Italian woman isn't,' she muttered with distaste.

'In this case, it is,' he insisted. 'One day three men walked into my office in broad daylight and told me I'd been messing around with a very important man's daughter, who already had a husband. I was warned that if I wanted to stay alive and prosper I had to get out of Fiorella's life.'

'Really?' Gwenna only registered that her father had been indulging in an affair with a married woman and she thought it served him right if he had for once been called to account for his behaviour. 'Maybe my mum would have had a happier life if she'd had a father capable of pulling the same stunt.'

'For heaven's sake, Gwenna. They put a gun to my head—I thought I was going to die!' Donald Hamilton protested furiously. 'They were violent criminals.'

'I'm sure,' Gwenna sighed, wondering where the tall tale would go next.

'I was managing Fiorella's money and she was a wealthy woman. Her father's thugs demanded that I hand over all of that money. They escorted me to the bank and waited while I made arrangements to withdraw her cash. But she'd already spent a good deal of it and the men threatened to come back and visit me a third time if I didn't cover the amount that had been spent. I had to pay up. They bled me dry. Needless to say I cut loose fast from Fiorella, but I was financially ruined.'

'I'm sorry… I don't believe any of this and I don't know how you can expect me to.'

'Your mother's solicitor worked in the same practice as I did. He was elderly, overdue for retirement. It was easy to remove papers from his safe,' the older man admitted. 'I approached a loan company in London and pretended I owned the Massey estate. Using it as security, I borrowed a large sum of money. I had to have some way of meeting my obligations at home. Remember you and your mother were my dependants then.'

Gwenna frowned, finally grasping the connection, even if she didn't credit the preceding story. 'How could you do that to my mother? Was she just one more person to be used and fleeced? Is there anyone you won't use?'

'When your mother died, there was still an outstanding loan against the estate and I had to cover up the evidence of that. What choice did I have? I may have forged that will but I did it with the best of intentions. I had such wonderful plans.'

A ragged laugh fell from her lips. 'Mum wanted me to have the estate, not you.'

'I gave you a home,' her father reminded her without hesitation. 'I hoped to develop the estate and you would have benefited from that too, if it had come off.'

'I don't think so. I was just a means to an end and a cheap

way to keep the nursery going.' Gwenna lifted the file and got up on stiff legs.

'You can't leave like this. What's going to happen now?' Vaulting to his feet, the older man skimmed an apprehensive glance out the window.

She followed his gaze. Angelo was leaning up against the long gleaming bonnet of his ridiculously sumptuous car. She realised that she didn't care what action Angelo took over her parent's most recent act of fraud. Presumably Angelo would relish the opportunity to prosecute him. That was fine by her but it also meant that her private agreement with Angelo would be null and void. Her father would be arrested and charged and he would go to court. And if she could not or would not intervene that meant that she was free again, as free as a bird, she registered numbly.

'*That's* Angelo Riccardi?' her father queried, his frown deepening. 'He looks younger than he does in newsprint. He reminds me of someone. Why don't you invite him in?'

'I don't want to,' she admitted without apology.

She walked out to the kitchen, grabbed the keys to the old four-wheel drive and went straight out to the yard at the back. She drove round the house, braking to a halt beside the limo before she could lose her nerve. With clumsy fingers, she frantically lowered the creaking window.

The epitome of cool, Angelo elevated an enquiring brow. 'Is that a roadworthy vehicle?'

'Don't be a snob,' Gwenna breathed tightly. 'Well, I suppose this is it. Our arrangement is over.'

Disturbed by the hollow, unfocused look in her eyes, Angelo cut in. 'Over?'

'You can press charges against my father. I don't care any more.'

His dark, lustrous eyes glittered. 'You don't mean that—'

'Yes, I do. He's a horrible man,' she said flatly. 'I'm certainly not going to sacrifice my life to keep him out of prison, so go ahead and prosecute him.'

'I wasn't referring to your father. It's the, "over" angle that I was questioning,' Angelo countered with pronounced care. 'You and me…'

Gwenna stared out the windscreen, her classic profile pale and tight. 'There is no you and me,' she whispered.' There was an arrangement and now it's finished. If the will was forged, the Massey estate is mine and just as soon as the legal work's done and your staff move on, I'll be taking over there again.'

'This is not the place to stage this discussion—'

'I don't have to discuss it. You can keep the clothes and forward the rest of my stuff to the nursery.' With that final assurance, Gwenna angled her vehicle round the nose of the limo and sped off down the drive.

Angelo was thunderstruck by the turn of events. She had taken him by surprise. How had that happened? Why hadn't it occurred to him that she might walk away once she stopped caring about what happened to her father? When had he lost his grip to that extent?

Piglet appeared round the corner of the house and ran past him in frenzied pursuit of Gwenna's old banger of a car. Left behind, the little dog had had a hair-raising encounter with the white Persian who ruled the Hamilton kitchen and he had fled through the cat flap.

For about ten seconds, Angelo stared after the dog in frowning surprise, and then, seeing the distraught little animal charging right out into the road, he unfroze and sprinted down the drive. Shouting at his team, Franco took off after him. The older man reached the roadside just in time to see his employer make a dive for Piglet, who was running frantically through the traffic. Scooping the little animal up, Angelo tossed him onto the grass verge and almost lost his balance in the process. As he rocked back on his heels, he was clipped by the wing of a car. Flung up over the bonnet, he came crashing down again to the accompaniment of squealing brakes and strident shouts. He lay still on the road, blood seeping from the side of his head. Shaking and whining with fright, Piglet sought security from the only familiar face and darted nervously into the shelter of Angelo's body to lick at his hand.

Gwenna had almost driven right through the village before she realised that she had not a clue where to go. At first she did not want to think about anything that had happened that morning. Every thought seemed laden with the threat of hurt and she felt curiously unable to cope even with the comparatively minor decision of where to go next.

The familiar sight of the Massey Manor gates took care of that concern for her. That part of the estate was closed to vehicular traffic and she parked outside, scrambling out to walk up the rough lane that had once been the entrance drive to the house. For the first time she wondered if her inability to think and react normally related to shock. Shock at her father's treachery and greed?

Shock at the revelation that she was, after all, the rightful owner of the estate that had been in her family for generations? Of course that fact would have to be ratified by a court of law before it was officially hers but, even so, it was good news, wasn't it? Nobody would ever be able to take the estate away from her again and in her hands it would be safe. The plant nursery would belong to her once more. It had made a reasonable income. When she was no longer required to pass over all the profits to her father, she would be able to build up the business and look forward to more comfortable takings in the future.

Perhaps, she finally conceded, she was also a little bit in shock at the concept of a life that no longer contained Angelo. How had he managed to become so entwined with her every thought and expectation? Why could she not imagine a future without him? Her mind served up a compelling image of Angelo. Aggressive and dynamic, he lived and moved at a fast pace. His electric energy, high expectations and impatience were symptomatic of his genius. He was only still and silent when he was asleep. At last she let herself contemplate the prospect of never seeing Angelo again and she realised with greater shock than ever that it hurt much more than anything else had that day. She pressed clammy hands to her tear-wet cheeks and sank down shakily on the worn sun-warmed steps of the old house.

When had she stopped hating Angelo? And why hadn't she realised that she had long since stopped hating him? How could she have fallen in love with Angelo? She fought all the time with him! He always knew best about everything! But she got quite a buzz out of fighting with him, didn't she? He was incredibly attractive and sexy and he made everything seem wildly exciting. Was it an infatuation? Well, she was soon going to have the chance to find out, wasn't she? She had just dumped him.

Could she change her mind about that? Would that be foolish? Pathetic? Or was it her duty to go cold turkey and get over him? Why, oh, why had she left her phone in the car? Suppose Angelo had called her?

It was at that point that Gwenna finally registered Piglet's absence and realised that she had left her pet behind at the Old Rectory. What a state she must have been in to walk out of there and just forget about poor Piglet! Rising upright and dusting down her dress, she went back down the lane and found Toby walking round her car and peering in.

'Looking for me?' she asked, unlocking the driver's door and immediately reaching for her phone.

'I was surprised to see your car parked here...'

There were a number of missed calls on her phone and she was about to access them to check out the caller when she noticed the odd note in Toby's voice. 'What's up?'

'I assumed you'd be at the hospital.' Toby was watching her closely for signs of reaction. 'You don't know, do you? Angelo's been involved in an accident.'

Her tummy flipped and her head swam. *Angelo...accident*. She stared at Toby in horror. 'An accident? Where? When?'

'Look, I'll take you to the hospital now.' Toby tucked her into the passenger seat of his low-slung sports car.

'Toby!' she prompted sickly. 'Just tell me!'

Toby drove out onto the road and cleared his throat. 'He was hit by a car—'

'You mean his car was hit—'

'Angelo wasn't in his car. It's possibly not the moment to mention it, but Piglet's all in one piece.'

'What's Piglet got to do with it?'

So Toby told her that Angelo had saved her dog's life. Angelo, who had once referred to her pet as a piranha fish on four legs. She felt sick with fear and horribly guilty.

Her mobile rang and she snatched it up. It was Franco. She was grateful for his calm but disturbed to hear that Angelo had still not regained consciousness. Having warned her that the press were gathering at the front of the hospital, Franco arranged to meet her in a less public location.

'I've told everyone that you're Mr Riccardi's partner,' Franco confessed, within a minute of their harried meeting.

Considering the connotations of that label and deeming them an outright lie in her case, Gwenna bit her lip. 'I don't think that…I mean—'

'That's the only way you'll be allowed to see him, Miss Hamilton. Lawyers are already on their way here to take charge.'

Gwenna stepped into the lift. *The only way you'll be allowed to see him.* The risk of being barred from seeing Angelo was quite enough to silence her qualms. 'Lawyers?'

'Decisions have to be made quickly about Mr Riccardi's treatment. You care about him. I trust you to make the right choices.' Franco looked grave. 'If you don't accept the responsibility, other interests could step in and take over here very quickly.'

Gwenna was startled by that warning, but she respected a candour that cut right through to what was really important. In the absence of family, Angelo's lawyers would hold sway and evidently Franco distrusted them. Angelo was hugely wealthy. Might that influence the quality of the choices made on his behalf? Gwenna didn't understand why Franco was so worried but she recognised his sincere concern for Angelo and hastily nodded agreement.

Franco guided her through a throng of people and into the presence of a harassed doctor, who was eager to issue a report on Angelo's condition. He thought Angelo's head injury should be scanned, which meant taking him to another hospital. But the lawyers were fighting over whether or not Angelo should be moved. Time was passing and the doctor was worried about the delay.

'Go ahead and make the arrangements for the scan,' Gwenna instructed.

'You'll take responsibility?'

'Yes, may I see him now?' Gwenna was struggling to contain her fierce impatience.

Angelo was pale, the side of his face cut and badly bruised and he was very, very still. She closed her hand over his limp brown fingers curled on top of the sheet. Swallowing convulsively, she sat down by the bed. Angelo had done a crazy but wonderful thing. And he could only have done it for *her* benefit. Wiping her eyes, she mustered a steadying breath and began to pray. Very few minutes passed before the nursing staff came in to prepare Angelo to be airlifted to a city hospital.

Angelo surfaced from what felt like the worst hangover of all time with a splitting headache. He was in the act of mastering a surge of nausea when he registered that a man was speaking in a sharp hectoring tone and that a hand was tightening on one of his as if he were a lifeline.

'I'm afraid you're going to hear my opinion whether you want it or not, Miss Hamilton,' the suave lawyer intoned with contempt. 'You let a junior doctor dictate a decision that may have seriously damaged Mr Riccardi's prospects of recovery.'

'That hospital didn't have the facilities to carry out a proper investigation. At that point, I felt that there was no time to waste.' Gwenna was wondering how many hours it was since she had last slept, for her head felt too heavy to be supported by her neck. Dawn light was filtering through the curtains.

'You acted without authority and with my express disagreement. Who are you? His *partner*?' the lawyer derided. 'You're the daughter of a criminal, and only one more in a long line of little—'

The thick black fringe of Angelo's lashes lifted to reveal the blazing impact of his gaze. 'Stop right there if you want to stay employed,' he growled hoarsely. 'Treat Miss Hamilton with respect. You do not abuse or bully her. Is that understood?'

Gwenna was only dimly aware of the other man's shaken apologies and immediate retreat. She was so overjoyed that Angelo had recovered consciousness that she was incapable of appreciating anything else. Her eyes filled with tears of relief. 'I was scared you were never going to wake up. I'll ring the bell for the nurse.'

'Not yet.' Angelo surveyed her, taking in the tousled honey tumble of her hair, her mascara-smudged-and-shadowed eyes and her unflattering pallor. He had never seen her look less beautiful and could not comprehend why, in spite of all the evidence to the contrary, she should look so wonderful to him. 'How long have I been out of it for?'

'Almost eighteen hours.'

She was still wearing the same clothes. Most probably, he reflected, she had not even looked in a mirror, for she was not vain. 'Have you been with me all that time?'

'Yes, of course.'

She had not left his side. She had sat up all night. He could not imagine a single woman of his acquaintance caring so little for her appearance or comfort and he was touched. 'You fought with my lawyers for my benefit. That was very brave,' he pronounced, retaining a firm grip on her hand. 'Did you shout at them?'

'No.'

'So, it's only me you shout at.'

Tears ready to overflow, she shook her head in wordless defeat at the over-emotional state she was in.

'It's a distinction that makes me feel special, *bellezza mia*,' Angelo declared, wondering why he liked the fact that she was crying over him.

Gwenna darted an uncomfortable glance at him and then lowered her lashes. 'After what I said, you must be wondering what I'm doing here.'

'You're here now,' Angelo cut in with the faintest suggestion of haste. 'Planning to go anywhere?'

And it was as if a door swept open in front of her without warning and he was already walking through it and away from her. The future had been static and unthreatening while Angelo was out for the count. Now life was beckoning again and the decision was hers. Yes to Angelo's question would mean turning her back on her misgivings and letting her heart guide her. If she listened to common sense, she would tell him no. She did not know if she could ever forgive him for the way things had started out. But the alternative was to leave him and she could not face that. Love, she was discovering, was much more complex than she had once fondly believed and it had stolen her freedom of choice.

'I still want you to come to Sardinia with me,' Angelo imparted huskily. 'I'm not putting any pressure on you. You owe me nothing.'

But she only had to look at that lean, dark, devastating face to feel the magnetic pull of the pressure he exerted without even trying. When he said that she owed him nothing he was coming as close as he was prepared to come to the fact that he had plunged her into a highly immoral arrangement. But he wasn't saying sorry and he probably never would. Yet she still needed him, still wanted him, she acknowledged guiltily. At that moment nothing else mattered. With a preliminary knock the consultant and his staff strode in. She had to give up her seat to let them carry out their checks on Angelo but his brilliant dark gaze did not stray from her.

'I'm waiting for an answer,' he told her as if they were still alone.

And she gave the only answer she could give.

His villa rejoiced in a stunning site on the limestone cliffs of the Golfo di Orosei. The property was surrounded by vibrantly colourful tropical gardens. A twisting secret path hedged in by vegetation led down through a grove of ancient cork oaks to a private beach of white sand. The magnificent house was staggeringly opulent. The overhanging roof, natural stone walls and wood floors kept the interior cool while huge comfortable sofas heaped with cushions made it inviting.

'And *this*…' Angelo trailed out the word with purring satisfaction at the conclusion of the grand tour '…is the master bedroom.'

At the press of a button, the wall of glass that overlooked the sunlit stone veranda split into two sections that slid back into recesses at either side. A hint of a breeze sent the diaphanous drapes fluttering. Gwenna strolled out to enjoy the dazzling view of the Mediterranean. In the sunlight, the sea had a sparkling turquoise brilliance.

'I'm in paradise,' Gwenna sighed, revelling in the warmth of the sun on her skin. 'I love the sound of the waves. It's so soothing. Mum used to have a friend with a house at the beach and when we went to visit we stayed over. I used to fall asleep listening to the surf.'

'How well do you swim?'

'Like a mermaid…why do you never mention your family?' Gwenna asked abruptly.

His lean body tensed as he closed his arms round her. 'What is there to say? After my mother died, I stayed in foster homes between school terms. I never knew my father.'

'That's a shame.'

'Think of the grief your father has caused you, *cara mia*.'

'That's true.'

Angelo turned her slowly round. Dark eyes smouldering beneath his black lashes, he dropped a kiss on top of her head.

He tugged loose the ties on her lace top. The heady strength of anticipation made her breath catch in her throat. Heat was slowly uncoiling in her pelvis, sending out wicked little tendrils of sensual awareness to every part of her.

The burn of his gaze on her nakedness made her tingle. Her legs went weak and he lifted her to carry her over to the bed.

'I apologise…that was a little rough and ready, *bellezza mia*,' Angelo groaned, studying her with melting tawny eyes that were slightly dazed.

Gwenna gave a delighted little shimmy beneath him and hugged him tight. If that was rough and ready, she could only look forward to refined.

Angelo tipped up her face. 'I mean it. That was more of a quick snack than the banquet I planned.'

Noting that the bruises were fading fast from his temples and cheekbone and feeling incredibly tender towards him, Gwenna grinned up at him.

'I wanted you to know how much I—'

'Missed me?' she slotted in buoyantly.

'How much I appreciate you,' Angelo contradicted a shade stiffly, beautiful eyes guarded, for it felt like a major statement to him.

Smothering a yawn, Gwenna let her eyelids drift down. 'I'm so sleepy.'

Angelo stared down at her in frustration. 'I *really* appreciate you…'

'Whatever,' she mumbled, drowsily unimpressed.

CHAPTER TEN

GWENNA threw a stick for Piglet to fetch as she walked along the beach. Four weeks of perfect relaxation and contentment in Sardinia had put a healthy glow in her cheeks and a spring into her step. She had got her peace of mind back and the silliest things made her smile, she reflected cheerfully.

Angelo had shamelessly bribed his way into Piglet's affections with chocolate treats. It had amused her that Angelo, so hopelessly competitive in every way, would not settle for mere tolerance from her pet. Piglet now adored Angelo and one of his favourite spots to sleep was below Angelo's desk. Unfortunately Angelo did not appreciate Piglet's amazingly loud snores.

She was very happy, but occasionally a cold chill would run over her when she considered the inevitable end of the affair. Nothing lasted for ever and she knew it. He was sure to get bored with her. She couldn't believe that she had what it took to hold his attention much longer. But she was determined to live for the moment…

Sometimes they were very active and she had been sailing, windsurfing and scuba-diving, not to mention dancing all night at a couple of exclusive clubs and at a much less exclusive street carnival. She had cheered at a horse race and had got embarrassingly tipsy at a peach festival, an instant of mistaken judgement that Angelo was prone to mentioning more than she liked. They had eaten out in tiny restaurants in inland villages where tourists were still rare and she had fallen madly in love with cheese and honey pastries. Occasionally, however, they had gone no further than their bedroom or the beach, and she had fallen asleep in his arms and wakened still in them for Angelo no longer left her to sleep in a bed of his own.

Slowly but surely she had come to recognise that he was truly making an effort to please and entertain her. He seemed gloriously unaware of the reality that she found just being with him a joy. He gave her flowers. He bestowed a jewelled collar and toys on Piglet. He ordered the food she liked best when they stayed in. He had said, rather touchingly, that he hoped it would be all right to buy her diamonds for her birthday. As that was still two months away she had been secretly overjoyed by that evidence of forward planning and stability…

The newspapers had been delivered at nine and, from the instant that Angelo saw the first headline, he was flooded by negative uneasy feelings. Blanking them out, he finally threw the papers aside and went outside to take some much-needed fresh air. He used binoculars to locate Gwenna, checking the shrubberies first and smiling at the reflection that his gardeners had been very more active since her arrival.

On this occasion, however, she was on the beach larking about with Piglet like a kid. Dressed in blue polka-dot shorts and a lemon sun top, she looked delectable. His shapely mouth compressed. She was solid gold. Unspoilt, honest and kind, as well as being the first woman to value him more than his wealth. Of course there was that guy, Toby, but Angelo had noticed that references to him had become a rarity. In any case he resolutely avoided recalling that awkward angle because, in every way that mattered, Gwenna Massey Hamilton was his. Possession was nine-tenths of the law, he reminded himself staunchly.

But sometimes as now, when disquiet put him into a more contemplative mood, Angelo was seriously spooked by what he had done to Gwenna. Once or twice he had endeavoured to get himself to the point of discussing his attitude to her when they had first met, but he had not known what he could possibly say. He knew that what he had done was unpardonable and he was just as aware that she had a lot of heart and not a spiteful bone in her beautiful body. Unfortunately, he was equally conscious of her principles, her outlook on the world, her essential trusting innocence. How could she forgive betrayal? Or cruelty? How could she ever understand a desire for revenge that had got out of hand?

He couldn't possibly tell her the truth. It wasn't his fault that his family tree was full of gangsters. But it *was* his fault that he had acted like one. He did not feel it would be wise to admit that he was haunted by the fear that there *was* such a thing as bad blood and that he had inherited it in his genes. After all, he had treated her badly and, put in possession of those facts, might she not understandably decide that he was a total bastard? And even if he reasoned fiercely, there was no reason why she should ever have to know. A leopard could change his spots—at least into the stripes of a tiger.

Gwenna noticed that Angelo was unusually quiet over dinner. There was a distant aspect to his lustrous dark eyes. Although he rarely touched alcohol, he took a brandy out onto the veranda without inviting her to join him. So, he was having an off-day, acting human, maybe even keen to escape the incessant chatter she occasionally directed at him, she reasoned ruefully. She was annoyed that she was being so over-sensitive and when he went down to the beach she resisted the urge to follow him. To occupy herself she lifted the newspaper he had been studying. It was a lengthy article about the life of a Mafia don who had died in South America. She took it to bed with her and ended up reading every word of the ghastly riveting stuff.

'What are you reading?'

Startled, Gwenna looked up and focused on the tall dark male poised beyond the circle of the lamplight. 'Angelo… where have you been?'

'You sound like a wife.' His dark voice was slightly slurred.

'If I was your wife, I'd have phoned you and asked you where you were and exactly when you would be back,' Gwenna admitted without hesitation.

Angelo flung back his cropped dark head and laughed with raw amusement. 'I like your candour, *cara mia*.'

In a black designer shirt and jeans, with his masculine beauty enhanced by stubble, Angelo looked mean, moody and magnificent. Her heartbeat speeded up. He threw himself down on the bed beside her and tapped the paper she had cast down. 'So, you're reading about Carmelo Zanetti…'

'He was so wicked and yet he never went to prison for his crimes—'

'But he died in exile, alone and sick and despised.'

Gwenna blinked because she wasn't accustomed to Angelo showing a more sensitive side unless he could make a joke of it. 'There is that…' Glancing back at the article, she pulled a face. 'He was very good-looking when he was young, which is deeply creepy. Did you know he was originally from Sardinia?'

Angelo scrunched up the newspaper and thrust it clumsily off the bed.

'What on earth—?' Gwenna began.

He reached up and hauled her down to him, kissing her breathless with a hunger that could have burned out a bonfire. 'I need you,' he confided hoarsely. 'I really need you with me tonight, *bellezza mia.*'

Although he was far from sober, there was something in that appeal and the almost clumsy way he was holding her prisoner that melted Gwenna down deep inside. 'I'm not going anywhere,' she whispered, tracing one bronzed cheek-bone with tender fingers.

Before dawn, she wakened to see him emerging from the bathroom towelling dry his hair and she switched on the lights to study him with troubled blue eyes. 'Can't you sleep?'

His lean, darkly handsome face tightened. 'I have something to tell you,' he breathed abruptly. 'I've done some stuff you know nothing about...'

Gwenna went rigid and suddenly she didn't want to know what was wrong; she was afraid that any confession he made would haunt her for ever. She wanted to shove a brick in his mouth. Had he been with another woman? But, in the space of a month he had left her side for a total of just three nights and he had spent a lot of time on the phone to her those evenings.

Angelo had slammed the door shut on the secret room of sins concerning her inside his head. He was convinced there would be no profit and only loss if he risked walking the true confessions route. Instead he presented her with what he saw as good news, designed to alleviate her worries, protect her reputation and make her happy.

'I've paid off your father's debt to the garden restoration fund.'

Astounded by that announcement, Gwenna gazed at him

with wide blue eyes. 'That's not possible. I thought he was being prosecuted—'

'Prosecuting him wouldn't be a good idea. Your father has made a full statement confessing to the forgery of your mother's will. That's to protect you and I from any future claim he might try to bring. I've also signed over ownership of the Massey estate to you. This way the dirty linen stays hidden and nobody need ever know. The garden committee is delighted—'

'Obviously, but—'

Angelo sank down on the bed beside her. 'If your father goes to prison now that you own the estate, some people will suspect that you were involved in his thefts. Mud sticks, *cara*.'

Gwenna winced. 'I didn't think of that…but I did think that he should be punished this time.'

'Don't worry. He's an incorrigible thief. He'll be caught stealing again and I won't intervene,' Angelo asserted with a confidence on that score that she found ever so slightly chilling. 'This time around, however, I was thinking of you, and you don't deserve to suffer any more for his crimes.'

'Okay,' she muttered uncertainly, wishing he had waited until she woke up properly before tackling such a serious subject. 'But it means that you've lost thousands and thousands of pounds.'

Angelo shifted a smooth brown shoulder in remarkably casual dismissal. 'My choice.'

'But it's just not right that you should make a loss because you want to protect me.' Gwenna raked anxious fingers through her sleep-tangled honey-blonde tresses.

'It *feels* right, *bellezza mia*.' Angelo curved her back firmly into his arms and she rested her drowsy head back against his shoulder. 'Go back to sleep.'

Gwenna turned her head round so that her cheek rested

against him. He smelt of soap and the indefinable scent that was just him. With a drowsy smile she drifted back to sleep.

She wakened to the noise of a helicopter coming in to land and a phone ringing somewhere. It was almost lunchtime. She had slept in and was surprised that Angelo hadn't roused her. From the veranda she could hear voices speaking in Italian on the level below. It sounded as though Angelo had flown in staff to work. After a shower she put on a light skirt and top and wandered downstairs in search of Angelo. The ground floor office suite was jumping with activity. People rushed past her, hurrying between one room and the next, while phones seemed to be ringing incessantly.

'We need a massive piece of damage limitation,' someone was saying urgently in English. 'But it won't do the boss any harm in the market-place.'

Angelo was in his study and he was doing something she had never seen him do in their entire acquaintance; he was doing nothing. In spite of the obvious crisis he was staring into space, pale as death beneath his olive skin, his striking bone structure clenched into hard, forbidding lines.

Gwenna closed the door behind her. 'Please tell me what's wrong,' she pressed worriedly. 'It was wrong last night as well, but you were determined to act like everything was okay. Where were you? Did something happen?'

Angelo rose lithely upright. 'I had a couple of drinks and then went to the church and lit a candle for my mother. I got talking to the priest. That's why I was out so late.'

Surprise and relief assailed her. 'I could've come with you…'

'I needed some time to think. But events have caught up with me. I have to tell you what happened because that information is now in the public domain. It's in the papers, on the TV news, all over the internet.'

'It sounds important, but I'm sure that whatever it is can't be as bad as you seem to think. You seem…a little shocked,' she said gently.

Grim dark eyes rested on her. 'I'm angry and I'm bitter, but I am not shocked.'

Gwenna went the diplomatic route and nodded in agreement.

'And to explain, I have to go back a few years. When I was eighteen I was called to a lawyer's office and told who my parents really were. My mother had left instructions to that effect in her will,' Angelo volunteered flatly. 'Before she died she had already warned me that she came from a bad family, that my father was a dangerous man and that if they found out where we lived, they would try to take me away from her.'

Gwenna thought that such knowledge must have been a very frightening burden for a little boy to carry around with him. Introduced to that culture of secrecy and fear at a very young age, it was hardly surprising that he had matured into so reserved a character.

'Riccardi is not the name I was born with,' Angelo continued. 'In fact my mother changed our surname a couple of times after she came to England because she was afraid of being traced. She was running away from her heritage and I've spent my life denying it,' Angelo admitted harshly.

'What heritage?'

'My mother was Carmelo Zanetti's daughter and my father was the son of another crime family.'

It took Gwenna thirty seconds to work out what he was telling her and if she was aghast, it was not for the reasons he had expected. 'My word, that old man who died this week was your grandfather and yet you didn't trust me enough to tell me that. No wonder you were upset last night!'

'*Per amor di Dio!* I wasn't upset!' Angelo launched at her

in an immediate denial. 'He was an evil man and I didn't know him—we met only once when he was already dying.'

Gwenna saw that being upset fell into the same category as being in shock in Angelo's uncompromisingly tough expectations of himself. If he said it wasn't happening, he could avoid having to acknowledge that he had emotions. She could only imagine how disturbing he must have found that meeting with his grandfather. She would have put her arms round him if she hadn't known that such obvious sympathy would infuriate him.

'You may have despised the person Carmelo Zanetti was, but he was still a close relative and you've been on your own virtually since your mother died,' she reminded him gently. 'Who your parents were doesn't matter, though. What you are inside is more important.'

'And where did you pick up that piece of worldly wisdom? Out of a Christmas cracker?' Angelo derided.

Gwenna stood her ground. 'What you do with your life matters more than your ancestry.'

Angelo vented a humourless laugh. 'Believe it or not, I wanted to be a barrister when I was eighteen. Once I found out that my entire family on both sides of the tree were involved in organised crime, I knew there was no way I could pursue such a profession.'

Drawn by his bitterness, Gwenna moved closer to him. 'That must have hurt.'

'It's immaterial. I had to know who I was to protect myself. I had to be careful who I trusted, who I did business with. I swore that everything I did would be legal and above board,' he breathed in a savage undertone.

'Of course you did,' she murmured softly.

'The same year the Zanetti family approached me through an intermediary with a job offer and a Ferrari car.'

Gwenna was appalled.

'I rejected the offer and ensured that I kept my distance. I should never have agreed to that meeting with Carmelo. It was the worst mistake I ever made,' he breathed grittily.

'Naturally you were curious.' Gwenna closed her hand over his in a helpless gesture of supportiveness. 'Don't be so hard on yourself. Obviously your mother tried to make a new life for both of you. But having to keep such a huge secret all these years must've put you under a lot of strain as well.'

Closing his arms round her, Angelo stared down at her with frank fascination. 'Have you put all this together in your head yet? Or are you still too busy trying to make me feel better?'

'Too busy trying to make you feel better. But I don't quite understand yet. You're annoyed because somehow your connection to Carmelo Zanetti has become public knowledge? How did that happen?'

'Carmelo decided to have the last laugh and he's blown my reputation sky-high,' Angelo volunteered heavily. 'The contents of his will have been leaked and I've been informed that he's left me all his worldly goods. In death he has made our relationship impossible to deny.'

'He must've had a soft spot for you…I mean, you're very successful and you didn't have to become a thug to achieve that. Making you his heir was probably his equivalent of boasting about you,' Gwenna contended in a positive tone, leaning into the hard shelter of his big tense frame and wishing he would relax a little.

'I also learned that it wasn't my mother's elderly former employer who financed my boarding-school education,' Angelo said bitterly. 'It was Carmelo. That makes me feel like an idiot!'

'I don't see why. You were only a child and people lied to

you,' Gwenna said sensibly. 'Did Franco already know that you have dodgy relations?'

'Not the details, but the reality that I had to take certain precautions about how I operate and who I employ close to me…yes.'

Gwenna recalled the older man's concern that what he had called 'other interests' might try to take control when Angelo was unconscious and unable to make decisions for himself. It dawned on her that Carmelo Zanetti, as a blood relative, might have demanded a say in the proceedings and she suppressed a shiver.

'Did your grandfather leave you much?' she asked as an afterthought.

'Millions…all clean and legitimate, according to his lawyer. I was the only close relative he had left. But I don't want his filthy money,' Angelo ground out with ferocious bite.

'Then you make sure that all that cash gets spent on really deserving causes. Cancer research, famine relief, Third World projects,' Gwenna suggested. 'Good can be made to come out of bad and nobody can fault you for that.'

Gazing wonderingly down at her serene face, Angelo was more than ever determined to take the story of his own involvement in her father's downfall to the grave with him. Not for one moment had she considered holding his ancestry against him. In addition, her inspired suggestion was the simple solution and the most appropriate to his predicament. His very highly paid PR consultants would not have dreamt of proposing that he give away that much money. But he didn't want it and putting that massive legacy to humanitarian use was the only way of acknowledging his unfortunate connections, while at the same time detaching himself from that taint.

Long brown fingers framed her cheekbone and his glinting

golden gaze was openly approving. 'You're a very special woman, *bellezza mia.*'

'Sometimes you take stuff too seriously. Rise above it all,' she urged. 'Remember that your mother rejected her family so that she could bring you up to lead a law-abiding life. Be proud that you've honoured that.'

His lean, powerful face shadowed. 'Law-abiding, *sì,*' he conceded sombrely. 'But I've still done things I'm not proud of.'

Someone knocked on the door and Angelo answered it. 'There's a phone call for you,' he interpreted as the maid spoke.

Less than pleased by the interruption at a point when Angelo seemed to be dropping the steel barrier of his reserve, Gwenna hurried past him. 'I'll be back in two minutes…don't go anywhere.'

Angelo smiled and then looked very surprised that he was smiling. Knowing that she had lifted his mood delighted her. It was a challenge for her to follow the maid into the next room when all she could think about was how much she loved him. Although she would never have dreamt of telling him the fact, she loved him all the more for betraying his vulnerability.

The sound of her father's voice on the phone made her tense in dismay. She supposed it would be too much to hope that he had not seen or heard some report of Angelo's origins. 'What is it?'

'Angelo Riccardi is Fiorella's son,' Donald Hamilton announced.

Gwenna was perplexed by that statement, for it came at her from an unexpected angle. 'Sorry, what are you saying?'

'Haven't you seen today's big story? Listened to the news? Don't you realise that your boyfriend is Don Carmelo Zanetti's grandson?'

'Yes, but…this Fiorella lady you mentioned—'

'She was Zanetti's daughter, but she wasn't calling herself Riccardi when I knew her. I only saw Angelo a couple of times when he was a toddler. Fiorella always left him with a babysitter,' her father informed her. 'Remember me saying that Angelo put me in mind of someone that day he got hit by the car?'

'Yes.' Gwenna was finding it hard to catch her breath and her legs were feeling all wonky. She backed down into the nearest chair. A past connection that close between her family and Angelo's? How could that be possible?

'Don't you see what this means?'

Her brain felt as if it were drowning in sludge. 'What a very small world we live in?'

'You can't be that naïve. Obviously we have both been set up to take a fall. I ditched Angelo's mother and ran, and maybe life wasn't too good for her after that without her money or me. But it wasn't my fault!'

'What are you talking about?' she exclaimed. 'Why on earth would I have been set up?'

'You're my daughter and that must have been the ultimate power-play for Riccardi. He's been toying with us like a cat with mice before it goes in for the kill!' Donald Hamilton condemned bitterly. 'My recent bad luck is no coincidence. Riccardi buys Furnridge and suddenly I'm being accused of theft—'

'You were guilty of theft—'

'Use your brain. The minute I realised who he was I knew I had to warn you. He's out to settle scores. What is he planning to do to you? I let his mother down badly... All right, I admit it. But I had no choice,' he argued fervidly. 'At least I now know that the reason I'm living a nightmare is that Angelo Riccardi came into my life!'

'I think the people you've stolen from might have a different opinion on that. I'm sorry, I don't want to continue this conversation.' Gwenna replaced the phone handset on its base with a shaking hand.

She could not bear to think about what she had just been told. She was afraid that if she did she might lose control. But could Angelo have been using her, intending to hurt her all along? Before she could lose her nerve, she went back into his study.

'Was your mother called Fiorella?' she asked straight out.

Angelo froze as if she had drawn a gun on him. *'Sì...'*

Her tummy performed a nasty little somersault, because she had been so eager for him to tell her otherwise. Yet, somewhere in her heart of hearts, she already knew that, for once, her father had been telling the truth. 'Did you know that she had an affair with my father?'

'Santo Cielo—that was him on the phone, wasn't it?' Angelo could actually see the change in her. Her face had a tight, pained aspect and her normally clear eyes were dulled and wary. He had a horrible sick sense of inevitability and it paralysed him. He could not think of a single line of defence. He could still hear Carmelo's voice saying, 'Don't do anything foolish.' He knew that what he had done was much worse than foolish. He had hurt her, and he couldn't take that hurt back.

Gwenna moistened her full lower lip with a nervous flicker of her tongue. 'A month ago, Dad told me about Fiorella for the first time. I thought it was such a silly melodramatic story and I didn't believe a word of it. I mean—gangsters threatening to kill him, taking your mother's money and his—'

'What story?' Angelo broke in to demand.

She repeated it as well as she could remember. Angelo lost colour and stared at her with incredulous dark eyes. He swung away then and turned back just as quickly. 'If they stripped her of her money, it would've been a deliberate ploy to force her home to her husband. If that is the real truth—'

'Dad didn't know who you were when he told me. He didn't realise you were her son until the newspapers identified you. I think that for once he wasn't lying but, hey…you go question him yourself!' Gwenna slung in a low, shaking voice, the pain and the anger coming out of nowhere at her. 'You were so careful never to go near him until things started getting too complicated—'

Angelo flung up his hands and brought them down again in a slow, holding movement. 'Just calm down…'

'Did you set out to destroy my father?'

'That's a hard question to answer.'

Her nails dug into her palms and the sting of discomfort spurred her on. 'I deserve an honest answer.'

His eyes were very dark and stormy, and he threw up his hands and strode out onto the veranda.

Gwenna followed him. 'Angelo…please don't lie.'

'Don't do this…it'll rip us apart,' he breathed very low.

'You're ripping me apart right now!' she fired back at him chokily.

Releasing his breath on a hiss, he swung back to her. 'It was my belief that your father stole my mother's money and left her destitute—'

'No…that's not what's at issue here. You don't try and muddy the water with excuses. Did you deliberately target him?'

'Yes. I had him investigated and it was obvious that he was spending much more than he was earning. I took over Furnridge and sent in the auditors. That's all it took to uncover his embezzlement.'

She swallowed thickly. 'What about me?'

'You…' Angelo echoed hoarsely. 'I can't explain you. I saw you and it was like being hit with a sledgehammer. I would have done anything to make you mine. I swear that I didn't know you were *his* daughter until you came to the office to plead for him—'

'It gave you a kick, didn't it?' she condemned in disgust. 'When did you realise that it wasn't him you were hurting, it was me?'

'Do you think I'm proud of it? Do you think I'm so stupid I didn't realise that I was damaging you?' Angelo shot at her fiercely. 'But I was in too deep before I understood that and then I thought I could make it all right. I just didn't want to let you go—'

'I was your mistress,' Gwenna flung back between gritted teeth of self-loathing. 'That's all I've ever been.'

'No, we passed that point long ago. You put me through hell. You kept on trying to dump me—you came to Sardinia of your own free will.'

'Blame that on your fatal charm. Or maybe you brain-washed me. I obviously wasn't clever enough to see that I was just part of your revenge,' she muttered shakily. 'You weren't going to confess either, were you?'

'I didn't want to lose you,' he bit out thickly.

'You never had me to lose,' Gwenna lied, determined not to show her distress. 'But I can see now that you set out to own me. Replacing the garden fund money, giving me back the estate. What else was that about?'

Angelo was studying her with raw intensity. 'Not about owning you. You've had so little in your life...what it was about was putting you first, taking your worries away, making you happy, *bellezza mia.*'

Gwenna shook her head in vehement disagreement. She had booted all her soft, squishy feelings and optimistic hopes behind a mental locked door. She didn't want to fool herself. She didn't want be taken in by anything he might say. She knew that she loved him so much she had to be very strong to break free of his hold on her.

So, all of a sudden, she was making herself look at their relationship as it really was. Why had she refused to see that she was still his mistress? He had even contrived to ensure that she cheerfully accepted that demeaning role. The only commitment she had asked for was fidelity and in return she had a guy who *really* appreciated her. That was how much in love she was. Like her misguided mother before her, she had settled for less because she was willing to take him on virtually any terms. Flailing herself with that humiliating belief, Gwenna stalked forward and crouched down to haul Piglet out from beneath Angelo's desk.

'As soon as it can be arranged, I want to leave and go home.'

'The press will eat you alive if you're linked with me now,' Angelo warned her tautly.

Gwenna hugged Piglet tight. 'If I can survive you, I can survive anything.'

Angelo watched her walk away and he did not know what to do. He felt like a man in a strait-jacket being tortured. The right words wouldn't come, yet *he* was a master of manipulation! He knew he could handle anything but, for some reason, he could not handle what was happening with her.

Gwenna beat to death a weed, hammering it into the ground until it was obliterated. Straightening, she sucked in a quivering breath and pushed her hair off her damp brow. Piglet was seated on the path looking anxious a good twenty feet away. Shocked by the turbulent emotions that kept on overwhelming her, she blinked back tears and took in another steadying breath.

It was only a week since she had seen Angelo, seven days of unadulterated hell and misery. Over and over again she kept on reviewing everything that had happened and everything that Angelo had said. He had not denied his guilt, which was in his favour, and he was hopeless at talking about feelings. But he hadn't fought to keep her either, had he?

Every time she thought about him she made herself recall that Angelo, who thrived on challenge and argument and scorching passion, had done nothing to stop her leaving him. Yet he was absolutely ruthless when he wanted to be. But he still hadn't tried to drag her off to bed to change her mind, or at least give her a proper chance to think over what she was doing. He hadn't threatened to hold her hostage or claim custody of Piglet. She could think of a dozen things he could have done to hang onto her—none of which he had done.

Twenty-four hours and the space to think over what had happened would have made a difference to her attitude, she reflected unhappily. For once she had begun looking back she had seen how much their relationship had changed and strengthened. Most importantly she had appreciated that Angelo had abandoned all thought of revenge when he chose to repay her father's depredations on the garden fund and sustained the loss of the value of the Massey estate without complaint. He hadn't cared that the downside of his generosity was that, once more, Donald Hamilton had escaped retribution. No, Angelo had indeed put her first. He had showed that he cared more about her peace of mind and happiness. That had been a big step for him. Only what did that matter now, and why did she keep on rerunning it all in her mind? In refusing to accept that Angelo had decided to let her go, she was driving herself crazy!

Piglet's tail began to wag and he charged off down the walled garden. When she called him, he ignored her. He had got very wilful since he had been spoilt rotten in Sardinia, she ruminated ruefully. He had also been very restless and excitable. The suspicion that he missed Angelo set her teeth on edge. She attacked another clump of weeds with her hoe.

Piglet's wild barking finally made her look up. Her dog was leaping and dancing in frantic welcome round the feet of the very tall, dark male striding across the grass towards her. Angelo, all potent masculinity and sophistication in a designer raincoat and a sleek business suit. As always, he was the living, breathing definition of drop-dead gorgeous. Her heart started thumping. She let go of her hoe and stepped off the soil onto the gravel path.

Angelo came to a halt ten feet away. His brilliant dark eyes roved over her in a hungry, all-encompassing appraisal, but there was a combative edge to his stance. 'I'm not leaving without you,' he intoned with cool resolve, 'but first you have to listen to what I need to say.'

Her mood had taken wings at that first declaration; however, she had too much pride to show the fact. 'You didn't have much to say when I left Sardinia last week.'

'I thought I deserved it. I was ashamed. I didn't know what to say to you.'

Her worried eyes brightened.

Angelo looked unusually pensive. 'Carmelo made a fool of me and who likes to admit that? I knew next to nothing about my mother. I only had a few memories. My enquiries met a brick wall and then I was invited to meet Carmelo and fill in the blanks.'

'So, of course, you went.'

'I took the bait. I was so arrogant, so sure I was incorruptible, but I was wrong,' Angelo admitted stonily and quietly. 'The old man reeled me in like a fish. He wound me up with the tale of how Donald Hamilton had seduced, robbed and dumped my mother when she was pregnant—'

'Oh…was she? Pregnant, I mean?' Gwenna questioned in consternation.

'Your father says no, but I'm not sure he could be trusted to give an honest answer on that score.'

Her eyes widened. 'You've been to see him…actually *talked* to him?'

'This morning. It was the sane thing to do. It's what I should've done when I first found out about him. Instead I tried to play God and I got burned.'

Gwenna was really impressed that he had been prepared to talk to her father but sort of cringing at the same time. 'What did you think of him?'

'He's very slippery with the truth, but he does tell a rollicking good story.' Angelo shrugged. 'I can't blame him for running like hell when he realised my mother was Carmelo's daughter and the wife of a Sorello. He's not hero material—'

'No, he's not.'

'He also swears that my mother knew he was already married, and how are we ever going to know otherwise? The truth is, it doesn't matter to me as much as it did. It's over and done with. Neither of them were saints.'

Gwenna had not appreciated just how badly his mother had been betrayed, or how deeply attached Angelo must have been to the image of the mother he had lost when he was still very young. 'But why did your grandfather wind you up about what my father had done?'

Angelo loosed a rueful laugh. 'Because he could; because it amused him. He saw that I believed I was different. I thought I was better than the tainted stock I came from—'

'Don't talk like that…you *are* better!'

'Carmelo still taught me a valuable lesson. Power and wealth corrupt.' Lean, powerful face taut with discomfiture, Angelo murmured curtly, 'I thought I was above the rules. I thought it was all right to use that power to expose your father—'

'And then you thought it was all right to use your power over him to have me,' she completed tightly.

'Will you ever forgive me for that?' Angelo asked gruffly. 'I don't know.'

Angelo paled and shifted from one foot onto the other. 'I never wanted anything as much as I wanted you…no woman, no deal, no prize ever exerted that much of a hold on me. You're in a class of your own, *bellezza mia*.'

'I'm not denying that, for some weird reason, I found you very attractive too,' Gwenna allowed, softening a little because he really did look miserable.

'But I didn't treat you properly. I was very stubborn. I couldn't understand why you couldn't be happy with what other women had accepted. But I didn't want you to be like them—in fact I wanted you because you were different.'

Gwenna finally grasped why he had sought her out again and her heart sank like a stone. 'You're here to tell me that you're sorry.'

Shimmering dark golden eyes collided with hers. 'But not sorry to have met you or known you. I can never regret that. I'm sorry I screwed up. I'm sorry I kept the truth from you. I'm sorry I hurt you,' he told her urgently. 'But right from the start I wanted you to love me and want me the way I believed you wanted Toby.'

Tears burned the backs of her eyes and she blinked fiercely. 'I was lying when I said I thought about him when I was with you.'

Angelo loosed an uncertain laugh. 'Now she tells me. You put me through hell.'

'I couldn't help it.'

'You kept on dumping me, but if you give me the chance I'll spend the rest of my life making you happy.'

Gwenna studied him fixedly. 'Seriously?' she enquired a tad shrilly, for she was very much afraid of misinterpreting what he was saying.

Without batting an eyelash, Angelo got down gracefully on one knee. 'Will you marry me?'

Gwenna was so astonished that she couldn't find her voice at first. He was asking her to marry him. *He was asking her to marry him!* Her Delft-blue eyes shone. She struggled to think of all the questions she should ask before coming to a decision and then decided not to bother, because there was absolutely no doubt in her mind about what her answer had to be. 'Yes…'

Angelo sprang upright, surprised at the speed of her response but content not to question it. 'Does that mean you forgive me?'

'Not necessarily…but I will marry you.' Gwenna discovered that her teeth were chattering with shock.

'Okay,' Angelo pronounced, wondering if that dazed look was positive or negative, and then remembering what he had not yet said. 'I love you…I love you a lot, *amata mia.*'

Dazzled by the enormous sapphire and diamond ring he'd placed on her finger as he confessed his love, Gwenna lifted startled eyes to his lean, darkly handsome face. 'You don't have to say that if you don't mean it.'

Angelo strode forward and caught both her hands in his. Intense tawny eyes claimed hers in a look as possessive and urgent as his hold. 'I can't sleep at night without you. When you left Sardinia I thought my life was over. I've been in love with you for weeks and weeks without realising it… I really need you to be with me…for ever.'

Overwhelmed, Gwenna nodded several times and squeezed his fingers and whispered fervently, 'I love you too…'

'What about Toby?' Angelo enquired with forced lightness of tone.

'I think I was just really scared of falling in love,' she confessed with an embarrassed grimace. 'It wrecked my mother's life, and Dad has a dreadful track record. Perhaps believing that I still loved Toby when I couldn't have him made me feel safe—'

'So, you're *over* him?' Angelo checked, not quite sure what he was being told, but hauling her up against his hard, muscular length just the same. 'Like, *totally* over him?'

'I love him as a friend… You know, I never did fancy him the way I fancied you.' Gwenna dropped that news in a self-conscious whisper. 'There's times when I can't wait to rip your clothes off.'

'I know the feeling, *amata mia*,' Angelo agreed raggedly, long, tanned fingers skimming through the layers of her jacket and her T-shirt to find the smooth skin of her slender waist.

Gloriously happy and quivering with the hot pulse of excitement that he always aroused, Gwenna wrapped her arms round him. 'I'm all muddy,' she muttered apologetically.

'I'm not fussy,' Angelo confessed, covering her luscious pink mouth with his, and groaning with sensual satisfaction when she responded with the abandoned enthusiasm that had made him her biggest fan.

From the gallery above the classic Regency hall of the Massey Manor, Angelo watched with amusement as the assembled members of the press tried without success to catch a photo of Gwenna either standing still or even looking in their direction. Having posed earlier that day to mark the official opening of the gardens, she had had quite enough of the cameras.

A glittering charity benefit in aid of a children's hospice

was being staged in their exquisitely restored English country home. In fact, a whole busy calendar of such events had been organised by the Rialto Foundation, the charitable trust established with Carmelo Zanetti's legacy. Angelo and Gwenna were giving as much time as possible to the foundation and it had been well supported by the media, who had been well impressed by Angelo's surrender of that amount of money.

Angelo thought that Gwenna was looking ravishingly beautiful in her pale blue evening dress, with sapphires and diamonds flashing at her throat and ears. He was very proud of his wife. In two years of marriage she had overseen the restoration of both house and gardens, travelled all over the world with him and acquired the name of being a wonderfully laid-back hostess. She also wrote a regular gardening column in a Sunday newspaper. He was the envy of many men.

But the greatest gift that Gwenna had given him apart from herself and her love was the lively little bundle Angelo was cradling against his shoulder. She had been christened Alice Fiorella Massey Riccardi, a giant moniker for a tiny baby. Six months on, they called her Ella. Angelo had been totally unprepared for the instantaneous attachment he had experienced the first time his daughter was placed in his arms. Piglet trotting at his heels—for Piglet did *not* like large crowds—Angelo took Ella back to her nanny in the nursery and laid her down in her cot. It was time to go downstairs and escort Gwenna onto the floor in the ballroom for the first dance.

'It's been a long day. I can't wait to have you all to myself, *amata mia*,' Angelo confided as he closed his arms round her.

A delightful quiver of anticipation rippled through Gwenna's slight frame. He was so demanding, she thought blissfully. She knew she was a very lucky woman. Whirled round the floor below the magnificent Venetian glass chande-

liers, she nestled closer to her husband's lean, powerful body.
It was a wonderful evening.

After she had said goodbye to the last of their guests she
shooed Piglet out of the dining room. 'You're getting fat,' she
scolded, lifting him away from the plate of cake he had discovered lying beneath a chair. The little animal was assuming
an even more barrel-like shape.

She went upstairs and checked on Ella, beaming down at
her darling rosy-cheeked daughter with her riot of black curls.
She had to admit that her pregnancy had come as a surprise.
In fact Angelo had been teasing her about her weight gain long
before it had dawned on either of them that an impromptu bout
of outdoor lovemaking during the previous summer had borne
fruit. But they had found Ella so much fun that they were
planning to have another baby quite soon so that their
daughter would have a playmate.

Gwenna felt that life had been exceedingly kind to her. She
was busy and fulfilled and not even her problem father had
managed to put a check on the great joy of her marriage.
Admittedly, Donald Hamilton had proved to be an ongoing
source of concern. His second marriage had broken up in a
welter of acrimony. Forced to live in reduced circumstances
and shunned by former friends, the older man had drowned
his sorrows in alcohol. Gwenna had tried her best to help but
to no avail. She had been very pleasantly surprised when
Angelo had taken the trouble to intervene and succeeded
where she had failed. Within weeks, Donald Hamilton had
been attending regular AA meetings in clean, smart clothes,
and last month he had started his new job: advising on how
to detect fraud within Rialto.

'He'll have no access to money and he'll be watched like
a fox in a hen coop. His boss is an ex-policeman,' Angelo had

assured her when she'd voiced the fear that the temptation might prove too much for her parent. 'I believe your father has already come up with some useful ideas.'

Angelo strolled up behind her as she removed her last earring. He scanned her dreamy blue eyes in the bedroom mirror. 'What are you thinking about?'

She went pink, for she had been thinking how touched she had been that he had sorted out her father's problems purely for her sake. That, in her opinion, was the definition of real lasting love.

'You were chatting to Toby for ages this evening. Any old vibes for me to worry about?' Angelo enquired, utterly despising himself for voicing that question but unable to silence it. He got on great with Toby James, but he could never quite forget that Toby had once been a threat to his peace of mind.

'Angelo…we were talking about the drainage problem in the kitchen garden,' she proffered gently.

She spun round and he linked his arms round her.

'I'm much more exciting, *bellezza mia*,' Angelo murmured silkily.

'I know…' Her breath tripped in her throat as he cupped her hips and lifted her against him in a shamelessly erotic move that literally melted her from outside in.

'Drainage,' Angelo repeated in a genuinely pained tone of disbelief.

His kiss was sweet, honeyed intoxication and wonderfully sensual.

'I may not be creative in the garden—'

'You're awfully creative in other ways,' Gwenna pointed out breathlessly.

His slashing smile was her reward. 'Because I love you…in bed, out of bed, any place, any time—'

Gwenna let her fingers delve adoringly into his luxuriant black hair. She was filled with a glorious swell of happiness and contentment. 'I love you too.'

* * * * *

We hope you enjoyed *The Italian's Inexperienced Mistress* by Lynne Graham.
Share this book with friends and give the gift of romance to others. See page 186 to find some ideas for sharing your books, and make someone feel as special as you do.

Visit www.HarlequinCelebrates.com to download a FREE BOOK and experience the variety of romances that we offer.
Choose from 16 different stories for a total approximate retail value of $60.
From passion, suspense & adventure, paranormal, home & family, to inspirational, Harlequin has a romance for everyone!

Nicole knew she should return to the wedding reception, but to sit there and be the subject of that man's never-ending stares was beyond her.

Russell's eyes had been constantly on her. She'd *felt* them raking over her, burning into her.

She *felt* his presence before he spoke, her skin breaking into instant goose bumps.

"We meet again, Nicole," Russell said quietly as he materialized next to her. "What are you doing out here? You missed all the toasts and speeches."

"I had a headache," Nicole invented.

"Have you taken something for it?"

"Yes," she lied again.

"And?"

"I'm feeling better."

"In that case, would you like to dance?" he said, his blue eyes fastening hard onto hers again.

They were powerful, those eyes. And oh, so sexy.

"I…I think I'd rather stay out here," she replied somewhat shakily.

"That's all right. The music's loud enough. We can dance right where we are."

Before she could find some other excuse, he drew her into his arms.

"I'm sorry if I was rude to you the other day," he said softly as he began to move her back and forth in a slow, sensual rhythm.

Nicole swallowed but didn't say anything in return. A wild heat was rushing through her.

"I have a confession to make," he whispered. "From the first moment I saw you, I wanted you."

Nicole jerked back out of his arms, her eyes widening as they flashed up to his.

"I daresay you've had many men say that to you over the years," he added. "Please believe me when I say I don't make a habit of such rash declarations. I was sure that a girl as exquisitely beautiful as you are would already be taken. But your being here tonight, alone, indicates that maybe I was mistaken…" His eyebrows lifted questioningly. "Is there a lover or boyfriend in your life at the moment?"

Nicole managed to shake her head in the negative.

"Then I'm free to tell you that seeing you again tonight has done nothing to lessen my interest. In fact, I want you more than I've wanted any woman before in my life."

The passion in his voice, and in his eyes, both dazzled and dazed her.

"You take my breath away," he ground out, cupping her chin firmly with his right hand and lifting her mouth toward his rapidly descending lips…

* * * * *

Will Russell's vengeful seduction go according to plan?
Or will he have to go even further, up the aisle,
with Nicole as his bride?

Find out in THE BILLIONAIRE'S BRIDE OF VENGEANCE
by Miranda Lee, the first title in the
THREE RICH HUSBANDS *trilogy that follows*
the taming of three wickedly sexy Australians,
available September 2009
only from Harlequin Presents.

Eight new intense and provocatively passionate romances
are available every month wherever books are sold,
including most bookstores, supermarkets,
discount stores and drugstores.

Share the joy
of love and romance!

The Italian's Inexperienced Mistress is an intense and passionate romance, which you can share with friends, family, book club members or anyone you think would enjoy a provocative romantic read.

Here are some ideas
for sharing books:

◆ Give to your sister, daughter, granddaughter, mother, friends or coworkers.
◆ Host your own book club.
◆ Share the books with members of your community group or PTA.
◆ Bring them to your community center, retirement home or hospital and brighten someone's day.

OR

◆ Leave them for others to enjoy on an airplane, in a coffee shop, at the Laundromat, doctor's/dentist's office, hairdresser, spa or vacation spot.

Please tell us about your experience reading and sharing these books at
www.tellharlequin.com.

IN-STORE COUPON

HARLEQUIN® *Presents*

Intense and provocatively passionate love affairs set in glamorous international settings

Save $1.⁰⁰
on the purchase of
The Billionaire's Bride of Vengeance
by Miranda Lee
or any other Harlequin
Presents® title.

On Sale August 25

Coupon expires February 28, 2010. Redeemable at participating retail outlets in the U.S. only. Limit one coupon per customer.

5 65373 00076 2 (8100)0 11628

HPBAPCOUP

IN-STORE COUPON

HARLEQUIN *Presents*

Intense and provocatively passionate love affairs set in glamorous international settings

Miranda Lee
THE BILLIONAIRE'S BRIDE OF VENGEANCE

Save $1.00 on the purchase of *The Billionaire's Bride of Vengeance* by Miranda Lee or any other Harlequin Presents® title.

On Sale August 25

Coupon expires February 28, 2010. Redeemable at participating retail outlets in Canada only. Limit one coupon per customer.

52608823

HPBAPCOUP2

REQUEST YOUR FREE BOOKS!

2 FREE NOVELS PLUS 2 FREE GIFTS!

YES! Please send me 2 FREE Harlequin Presents® novels and my 2 FREE gifts (gifts are worth about $10). After receiving them, if I don't wish to receive any more books, I can return the shipping statement marked "cancel". If I don't cancel, I will receive 6 brand-new novels every month and be billed just $4.05 per book in the U.S. or $4.74 per book in Canada. That's a savings of close to 15% off the cover price! It's quite a bargain! Shipping and handling is just 50¢ per book*. I understand that accepting the 2 free books and gifts places me under no obligation to buy anything. I can always return a shipment and cancel at any time. Even if I never buy another book, the two free books and gifts are mine to keep forever.

106 HDN EYRQ 306 HDN EYR2

Name	(PLEASE PRINT)	
Address		Apt. #
City	State/Prov.	Zip/Postal Code

Signature (if under 18, a parent or guardian must sign)

Mail to the **Harlequin Reader Service:**
IN U.S.A.: P.O. Box 1867, Buffalo, NY 14240-1867
IN CANADA: P.O. Box 609, Fort Erie, Ontario L2A 5X3

Not valid to current subscribers of Harlequin Presents books.

Are you a current subscriber of Harlequin Presents books and want to receive the larger-print edition? Call 1-800-873-8635 today!

* Terms and prices subject to change without notice. Prices do not include applicable taxes. Sales tax applicable in N.Y. Canadian residents will be charged applicable provincial taxes and GST. Offer not valid in Quebec. This offer is limited to one order per household. All orders subject to approval. Credit or debit balances in a customer's account(s) may be offset by any other outstanding balance owed by or to the customer. Please allow 4 to 6 weeks for delivery. Offer available while quantities last.

Your Privacy: Harlequin Books is committed to protecting your privacy. Our Privacy Policy is available online at www.eHarlequin.com or upon request from the Reader Service. From time to time we make our lists of customers available to reputable third parties who may have a product or service of interest to you. If you would prefer we not share your name and address, please check here. ☐

Discover the
Harlequin® Romance novel
that's just right for you.

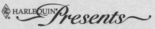

HARLEQUIN
Ambassadors

Want to share your passion for reading Harlequin® Books?

Become a Harlequin Ambassador!

Harlequin Ambassadors are a group of passionate and well-connected readers who are willing to share their joy of reading Harlequin® books with family and friends.

You'll be sent all the tools you need to spark great conversation, including free books!

All we ask is that you share the romance with your friends and family!

You'll also be invited to have a say in new book ideas and exchange opinions with women just like you!

To see if you qualify* to be a Harlequin Ambassador, please visit **www.HarlequinAmbassadors.com.**

*Please note that not everyone who applies to be a Harlequin Ambassador will qualify. For more information please visit www.HarlequinAmbassadors.com.

Thank you for your participation.